Out of Bounds

David C Robertson

To Laura,
with best wishes

David C Robertson

Out of Bounds

David C Robertson

Copyright © David C Robertson 2010

ISBN: 978-0-9565270-0-4

Published by David C Robertson
in conjunction with Writersworld Ltd
Printed and bound by www.printondemand-worldwide.com
Copy edited by Jeremy Renals

WRITERSWORLD
2 Bear Close, Woodstock, Oxfordshire, OX20 1JX, United Kingdom
www.writersworld.co.uk

CHAPTER 1

'Ben, it's time to get up. You'll be late for school.'
Ben Harper rolled over and pulled the covers up under
his chin. Outside his bedroom window, everything was
strangely still, smothered in a blanket of deep snow.

'If you don't get a move on, you're going to miss the
bus.' His mum's voice was louder this time, but
somehow Ben didn't really care. He didn't mind if he
missed the bus. If he just kept his eyes closed, he could
pretend it was the holidays and he didn't have to go to
school. Perhaps his mum had made a mistake. Just a few
more minutes in bed wouldn't do any harm.

It was the explosion that shook him awake. At first he
wasn't sure what it was, a dull thud somewhere high up
on the mountain. Then he heard the rumble of snow and
air as the avalanche hurtled down into a gully, out of

3

harm's way. His bedroom window shook. Ben leapt out of bed and pulled back the curtains. Outside large flakes of snow drifted down in the morning air. The white powder was piled up in deep drifts against the side of the house. The explosion could mean only one thing. His dad must already be up on the mountain, blasting away an overhang to make the ski area safe. There was a knock on his bedroom door.

'Who is it?' A small head looked in. It was his sister, Becky.

'Mum says if I'm late for school, you're going to get the blame.'

'Alright, alright, I'm coming.' Ben quickly got washed and dressed. By the time he got downstairs, Becky had almost finished her breakfast.

'Hurry up and sit down.' His mum put his breakfast in front of him. 'Your dad's been up on the mountain since first light. I don't want him to find you two still here when he gets in.' Ben's dad worked for the Forest Ridge Ski Patrol. This was the busiest time of the year, getting the ski runs ready for the new season.

'Where's Max?' Max was Ben's dog. Well sort of. He was a working dog and helped the Ski Patrol in search and rescue. Ben had looked after him since he was a puppy.

His mum nodded towards the back door. 'He's out the back. You'd better let him in before he digs up any more of my bulbs.' Ben went and opened the back door and looked out. Max had his nose buried in the snow. He had picked up the scent of something hidden in the ground.

'Max, here boy, come.' Max lifted his head, barked a greeting and came bounding towards the house. In an instant he was all over Ben, wagging his tail and trying to lick his face. 'Get down, you silly dog.' Max's nose and coat were covered with snow so he shook himself dry, all over the kitchen floor and all over Ben. 'Oh no, look what you've done now.' Becky thought it was really funny.

'Hurry up and finish your breakfast and don't feed him any titbits. He's got a job to do and he won't be able to work if he's overweight.' Ben sat down and slipped Max a piece of buttered toast under the table. His mum came and joined them, a cup of coffee in her hand.

'There's been a heavy build up of snow on some of the upper slopes over the last few days. The Ski Patrol has been using blasting charges to bring it down before it does any damage. They're hoping to get the slopes open this week.'

'I know,' said Ben. 'I heard the explosion.'

'So did I,' said Becky. 'I heard it first.' Ben raised his eyes to the ceiling.

'No you didn't. How could you hear it first? We both heard it at the same time. Honestly, Becky, you sometimes say the silliest things.'

'No I don't.'

'Yes you do, and anyway I'm two years older than you and I know best.' Their mum wasn't having any disagreement.

'You don't have time to argue. You had both better get your coats and boots on. The bus will be here in five minutes. Here are your backpacks. Your lunches are inside. Now come on, quick as you can.'

Outside the snow squeaked like talcum powder as they plodded through the drifts down the path to the road. Sam and Zoe were already there, huddled inside the bus shelter.

'Oh, here they come,' shouted Sam, 'late again.'

'You can talk,' said Ben. 'You missed the bus twice last month.' Sam laughed. He still enjoyed a joke despite everything. Sam lived with his dad in a small cabin on the outskirts of the village. Things had been difficult since his mum had died. His dad took work wherever he could find it. At this time of year, he helped keep the tows and chairlifts running.

'The bus is late,' said Zoe. 'It must be the snow.'

'Oh great,' said Ben. 'Maybe it has broken down and we can all have a day off school.' They all cheered.

Suddenly, a snowball whizzed past Ben's ear and splattered against the side of the bus shelter.

'Look out!' Ben turned around just in time to spot Marcus on the other side of the road before he ducked down behind a wall. 'We're under attack. Let him have it, guys.'

They all started pelting the wall with snowballs. Marcus kept his head down.

'Come on, let's see you,' shouted Sam. 'Do you give up?' A white hanky appeared above the wall, waving in mock surrender. They all cheered. Marcus stood up grinning.

'Okay, I surrender. What's happened to the bus?'

'It's late,' said Zoe.

'It has probably broken down,' said Becky.

'No such luck,' said Ben. 'It'll be here in a minute.'

Marcus crossed the road to join them. He was almost two years older than Ben, Sam and Zoe and a lot older than Becky. He went to the senior school down in Bridgeton. Marcus' dad owned the largest sports store in Forest Ridge so he always had the best gear - the latest skis and boots, the flashiest suit, and the classiest shades. You name it, Marcus had it.

A horn sounded somewhere down the road. Sam cheered. It was the bus. They gathered up their backpacks and waited patiently. Marcus pulled Ben to one side.

'Why don't you come with me?' he whispered in a low voice.

'Come where?' said Ben, puzzled.

'Down to Bridgeton, of course.'

'But I thought you were going to school.'

'Who said anything about school?' A strange look came over Marcus' face which made Ben nervous. Surely he wasn't thinking of skipping school?

'I can't,' said Ben. 'My mum and dad would find out. Becky would tell.' Ben was almost glad Becky would tell. What was Marcus thinking of?

'Okay,' said Marcus, 'if you don't want a bit of adventure, that's up to you.'

The bus swung around the corner, its snow-chains crunching on the frozen road. They all piled onboard and the doors swished shut. Ben watched Marcus through the bus window as it pulled away. He watched him cross the road to catch the return bus down to the valley. He had his hands stuck deep in his pockets, with his eyes staring at the snow. Ben couldn't help but feel Marcus was up to something.

CHAPTER 2

Ben's classroom was on the second floor of Forest Ridge Junior School. His teacher was Ms Curtis and this would be his final year before he would transfer to the senior school, down the valley in Bridgeton.

'Okay, everyone, make sure you all hang your coats up to dry.' Ms Curtis was waiting at the classroom door to welcome them. 'Come along, Ben. You don't need to take all day. We've got lots to do.'

Zoe and Sam were in the same class as Ben. Zoe sat at the table next to him and Sam sat near the front of the room where Ms Curtis could keep an eye on him.

'So, Ben, what was Marcus asking you to do?' Zoe didn't miss much.

'Eh, what do you mean?' Ben tried to sound casual.

'I can tell when Marcus is up to something,' said Zoe. 'What did he say to you before you got on the bus?'

'Nothing much. He just wanted to know if I fancied going down to Bridgeton sometime to have a look around.' Ben knew this wasn't the whole truth but he didn't want to get Marcus into trouble. Zoe gave him a long look.

'You know what Marcus is like,' said Zoe. 'He's always planning something.' Ben said nothing. They both knew Marcus had been planning something and it was more than just skipping school. Fortunately, Ms Curtis came in at that moment and told them to get their work out, so he didn't need to think of an answer.

It snowed all day and didn't ease up until after lunch. Ben couldn't wait for the holidays to come, so he could pick up his lift pass for the season and get his skis out again.

'Right, everyone,' said Ms Curtis, 'this afternoon, we're going to do some story writing.' Some of the children in the class seemed pleased whilst others groaned quietly. 'Zoe, would you please give everyone a piece of paper. Here you are. Make sure you don't miss anyone.' Zoe went from table to table handing out the paper. One or two of the children began to sharpen their pencils.

'Now, boys and girls, what do you think we are going to write about this afternoon?' Ms Curtis looked around the room. Sam put his hand up.

'The snow, Ms Curtis?' Everyone in the class laughed.

'Yes, Sam, we could write about the snow, but can you think of how we could make our story more exciting?' Zoe put her hand up.

'Could we write about an adventure in the snow, Ms Curtis?' said Zoe.

'That's a good idea, Zoe. Who can give me some interesting words we could use?' The class began to call out some words that they could use in their stories and Ms Curtis wrote them up on the board at the front of the classroom. 'Now, can anyone think of a good title for our story?' Ms Curtis moved around the room whilst all the children put their thinking caps on. She stopped beside Sam. 'Well, Sam, what do you think would be a good title for our story?' Sam was a bit taken by surprise. He'd been dreaming again.

'I've got it,' said Sam. 'The Abominable Snowman?' Everyone laughed. Even Ms Curtis smiled.

'I know, Ms Curtis,' said Zoe. 'We could write about an avalanche and call it Danger on the Mountain.'

Ms Curtis seemed pleased. 'What a good idea.' She wrote the title of the story on the board for everyone to see. 'Alright, boys and girls, Danger on the Mountain it is, and we're all going to write about an avalanche. Let's get started.' A hush fell on the classroom as everyone wrote down the title and made a start on their story.

From his seat in the corner, Ben could just hear the gentle tick of the wall clock which stood guard over the classroom door. It's large, clear face and hands showed just after two o'clock. In another hour or so school would be finished for the day. If only he could think of something to write.

It should have been easy - a story about an avalanche his teacher had said, and Ben knew all about avalanches; at least he thought he did.

'Come on, Ben, let's see if you can make a start.' Ms Curtis had stopped by his table and was looking over his shoulder at the blank page. 'I'm sure your dad has told you lots of stories about avalanches and dangers on the mountain.'

'I'm sorry, Ms Curtis. I guess I just find it hard to get started.' Ben knew this wasn't exactly true. He could write an exciting adventure story if he put his mind to it but he'd much rather be outside in the snow actually enjoying the thrills and spills at first hand. Ben picked up his pencil and thought about all the great times he'd had on the mountain.

The very first time he put on a pair of skis, he demolished a lift queue and ended up head-down in a stream. He was only six at the time which perhaps excuses him, although the people in the lift queue may not have agreed. As for the stream - well, Ben was convinced that it shouldn't have been there in the first place and, within ten minutes, he was back on the slope again.

Skiing soon became Ben's favourite sport and it got him into one or two hair-raising scrapes. Not that Ben was reckless. His dad made sure he respected the mountain and its dangers. However, try as he might, Ben could never resist the challenge to go one step further. Like the day he skied, with only one ski, all the way down from Crystal Rock, because someone said it couldn't be done. He took a few tumbles in the attempt but he proved them wrong all the same.

There was, however, one challenge that Ben could resist; one untried route that he would gladly avoid, even on the few occasions it was open for skiing. The Precipice run dropped almost vertically from the top of Eagle Summit. On a few days each season, its hard crust of sheet ice softened sufficiently for extreme skiers to venture onto its northern face. Ben could only marvel at their courage, or fool-hardiness, and felt a hidden fear rise within him.

But this of course was still term time and, ski resort or no ski resort, that meant school. Ben looked up from his blank page. The classroom had gone very quiet, a fish-bowl of concentration. Outside the double-glazed windows, it had started to snow again. Great white crystals of dry powder floated gently past the glass in the still, crisp air. It was minus ten Celsius outside. Ben had checked it on the playground thermometer at lunchtime. It was going to be a great season. Why, even now, the coaches and cars would be snaking their way up the twisting mountain road from the valley below, crammed with once-a-year skiers all seeking the thrill of the slopes. If only he could join them sooner.

Unfortunately, there was still one more week of school before they broke up. One more week before he and his friends could even consider attempting what they had secretly talked about during the summer.

It had been Marcus' idea really. He'd thought of it first. Ben, Zoe, Sam and Marcus had been poring over a map one day arguing, as usual, about who'd covered the most runs and which were the most difficult when, suddenly, Marcus said, 'Why don't we ski over to Silver Lake?'

At first, no-one knew what he meant. Silver Lake was the neighbouring resort. It lay in the next valley, about an hour's bus ride away by road. It was Zoe who spoke first. 'Don't be stupid. That's impossible.'

'Not if you know how,' replied Marcus. Ben had been friends with Marcus since they were little and he'd never known him to say anything he didn't mean.

'You can't ski over to Silver Lake from here,' insisted Zoe. 'It's not on. Anyone knows that.' Zoe was not the sort of girl to let any boy put one over on her. She knew the ski area better than anyone. Her mum managed the Edelweiss Restaurant next to the main lift station. She'd tried all the runs, many times, and there was just no way over to Silver Lake.

It was Sam's turn to chip in. 'She's right, the only way to Silver Lake is by bus or car.' Although he wasn't the brightest in the class, Sam was very practical and knew his way around the mountain.

'I think Marcus should be given a chance to explain,' said Ben. 'So, Marcus, tell us, how do we ski to Silver Lake?'

Marcus looked slowly around the group. 'We go by the glacier - right up to Eagle Summit and down the far side.' His voice was so steady and matter of fact when he said it, Ben knew he wasn't joking.

'Over the back of Eagle Summit?' Ben was almost speechless. 'You can't be serious. That's out of bounds. They'll never allow us.'

'So, we don't tell them.' Marcus stared at him. 'We just go for it. We could do it in a morning and be back before anyone noticed.'

At the time, Ben had been too taken aback to argue. Of all the dangers on the mountain that his dad had warned him about, going off the patrolled runs was just about top of the list. Skiing out of bounds was strictly for experts only, preferably with an experienced guide, not for children barely into double figures. Yet, as hard as he tried, Ben could not get Marcus' plan out of his head. It was crazy. It was unthinkable. But, then again, it had all the makings of an adventure that they could brag about for years, if only they dared to try it.

'Just a few more minutes, everyone,' said Ms Curtis, 'then we'll hear what you've all been writing about.'

Oh no. Ben suddenly realised he'd been day-dreaming. Was that the time already? He still hadn't written a single word.

'Okay, children, just put your pencils down. Don't worry if you haven't quite finished. You'll have time to complete your stories tomorrow if you need to. Would everyone please come and sit at the front of the class.' All the children shuffled out to the front and settled down on the carpet clutching their stories. 'Now,' said Ms Curtis, 'let's hear who's got the best avalanche story. I hope they're exciting. Ben, would you like to begin?'

For one terrible moment, Ben just wished the ground would open and swallow him up. 'Come to the front, Ben, where we can all see you. Don't be shy.' Everyone in the class was looking at him, eager to hear his story - his, as yet, unwritten story. For a moment Ben thought about making some excuse. He could say he felt sick. He could ask to go to the toilet. But it was no use. He'd have to own up in the end, so why delay the moment of truth. Ben shuffled slowly to his feet, braced himself and opened his mouth to explain.

But fortunately, or unfortunately, he never got a chance to speak. From somewhere outside the school there suddenly came the strangest noise. It was a swelling, rushing sound that Ben felt sure he ought to recognise. It started as a low distant rumble, muffled but somehow familiar, and quickly grew into what can only be described as a rising roar that came ever closer. For what seemed like minutes, but could only have been seconds, no-one uttered a sound. They all just froze, listening, trying to understand what was about to happen. And then it came …

'Avalanche,' whispered Ben. 'It's an avalanche!'

And with that, their whole world fell in. The walls of the classroom, seemingly so solid and secure, were suddenly shaken by a terrifying force; the floor trembled and lurched violently, and then, down through the roof, in an explosion of plaster and dust, crashed the twisted trunk of a gigantic fir tree.

It was all over in seconds. No-one even had a chance to scream. Where once there had been a ceiling over their heads, there was now a ragged gash and grey sky. Across the crushed tables, where they had been sitting just a few minutes before, lay the huge trunk of the tree, and down through the gaping hole drifted flakes of powdered snow.

How they all managed to survive without injury is something of a miracle. Perhaps it was on account of Ben's story, or lack of it. Who knows? In any event, one thing was certain. The school would have to close for the holidays sooner than expected.

CHAPTER 3

The day after the avalanche the grey skies cleared a little, and the sun appeared briefly between the passing clouds. A little group had gathered outside the school to see the damage for themselves. No-one could believe that everyone had escaped unharmed.

Workmen had erected safety barriers around the building and some official looking people in yellow jackets and hard hats were inspecting the damage. You could just see the roots of the giant tree trunk jutting out of the roof, and a landslide of rock, mud and snow had engulfed part of the playground. It had certainly been a lucky escape and it was going to take some clearing up.

Ben and Sam looked at where their classroom had been.

'What a mess,' said Sam. 'Do you think they'll be able to fix it?'

'Oh course they will,' said Ben, 'but it's going to take some time.'

'Oh, what a pity,' said Sam. 'I was so looking forward to another week of school.'

'Yes, I know,' said Ben. 'I'm going to miss it. What are we going to do?' Ben and Sam looked at each other and smiled. Just think, they had an extra week's holiday, three whole weeks to explore the mountain. 'Come on,' said Ben. 'Let's find the others.'

From the school, the main road wound its way up through the village as far as it could go, until it reached the gondola station. This was known as Forest Ridge Central, a large stone-clad building that housed the main lift system up the mountain. Next to it stood the ticket office and a large electronic display board which showed which runs were open.

'Let's check the weather forecast,' said Ben. Beside the ticket office was a board where they pinned up the three-day forecast for the ski area. They used little symbols to show if the weather was going to be cloudy, snowing or sunny. Ben and Sam studied it carefully.

'It looks like it will be partly cloudy tomorrow,' said Sam, 'and then sunny on Thursday with more snow on Friday. That's not bad.'

'Yes, as long as we can trust the forecast,' said Ben. 'My dad says it's difficult to predict how fast the weather fronts will move through. If the weather's good, it's always best to make the most of it. You never know when the next storm may sweep in and close the mountain down.'

'Come on,' said Sam, 'let's check out the Edelweiss Restaurant.'

The Edelweiss was the largest place to eat and drink in the village. Zoe's mum managed the restaurant so, with the school closed, there would be a good chance that Zoe would be there too.

A blast of hot air greeted them as the automatic doors slid open. There were already a few puddles on the tiled floor from the boots of skiers. As they'd guessed, Zoe was sitting in the far corner, by the window, reading a book. She had a mug of hot chocolate in front of her. She looked up and spotted Ben and Sam and waved.

'Hi, we thought we'd find you here,' said Ben. 'Have you picked up your season ticket yet?'

'No,' said Zoe, 'I was waiting for you two.'

Children whose parents worked in Forest Ridge were entitled to a free lift pass. It allowed them to ski anywhere on the mountain and in the neighbouring resort of Silver Lake. Last season they'd introduced a new computerised system with electronic gates. Once you had your lift pass you just needed to keep it safely in an arm or side pocket, and you could ride any lift or cable car, anywhere on the mountain.

'Hello, Ben. How are you, Sam?' It was Zoe's mum.

'Fine, Mrs Roberts. We've just come to find Zoe,' said Sam.

'Yes, we thought we'd go and collect our season tickets,' said Ben.

'Oh, I see. You're keen to get out on the mountain then. I can't say I blame you.'

Zoe's mum tidied some of the chairs. 'Just make sure you don't get into any trouble. Come back here for lunch if you like. Things are quiet at the moment. I'll give you a table in the corner and you can plan what you're going to do.'

Zoe put away her book and pulled on her coat. 'I'll see you later, Mum.'

Outside a snowplough swept by, pushing a mound of snow and slush ahead of it. In its wake it scattered a trail of salt and grit on the icy surface of the road. The ticket office lay next to the main lift station. They joined the shortest queue and waited their turn to be served. When Ben reached the cashier, he laid his school ID card on the counter.

'Good morning. I've come to collect my season ticket,' said Ben. The girl behind the counter took his card and swiped his ID number into the computer. His details appeared on the screen.

'Ben Harper?'

'That's me,' said Ben. The girl slid a blank lift pass into the electronic reader and programmed Ben's details onto the card.

'There you are. Make sure you don't lose it.' She passed his lift pass across the counter, along with a booklet on the terms and conditions of use and a map of the runs in Forest Ridge and Silver Lake. As he waited for Zoe and Sam to be served, Ben zipped the lift pass into the left arm pocket of his ski jacket and had a quick look at the terms and conditions of use. One section in bold print caught his eye:

It is strictly forbidden to ski outside the patrolled ski area. Any misuse of the terms and conditions may result in the ski pass being withdrawn.

Ben carefully zipped the booklet and map into his inside pocket. When Zoe and Sam had collected their lift passes, they all went outside to check the electronic display board to see which runs were open. The Snowcat machines had been working flat out grooming the slopes and getting them ready for the new season. Already half of the runs were open. Work would continue all through the night so, by tomorrow, most of the mountain would be skiable.

Over the next few weeks Forest Ridge would start to fill up with holiday makers. The shop windows which lined the main street were already stocked with ski clothing, boots and equipment, all in the latest colours, styles and branding. Outside the Chocolate Box, on the corner, they stopped to look at the mouth-watering displays. Behind the curved glass windows were trays of fine, handmade chocolates; some dark, some light, but all of them sweet, rich and delicious.

Crossing over the road, they passed the outdoor skating rink where some children were already taking advantage of the early holiday. They watched as the skaters whizzed around the ice, some on their own and some holding hands. Others were just sitting on the frozen surface where they had tumbled. This was the place to come in the evenings, after dark, when the ice was brightly lit with coloured lights and loud music blared out from the speakers at the side of the rink.

'Let's come here some evening,' said Zoe. 'We can hire ice-skates for an hour.'

'Okay, you're on,' said Ben. 'I bet I can skate faster than you.'

Nearby was the swimming pool where they used to go to have lessons when they were little. The water was always warm because it was fed from hot springs deep underground. From the indoor pool you could swim, under a canopy, to the outdoor pool which steamed in the cold air. Some children were playing in the outdoor pool, daring each other to climb out onto the side and roll in the snow.

'I fancy doing that,' said Sam. 'Who wants to roll in the freezing snow?'

'No way,' said Zoe. 'You're not getting me to do that.'

Ben laughed. 'What not even if we dared you?'

'Not even if you dared me. I'm not stupid,' said Zoe.

For the rest of the morning the three of them toured around the stores trying on hats and gloves and backpacks. Sam bought a detailed map of the surrounding area which showed all the paths and routes you could take on the mountain during the summer months. The map he had used all last summer with his dad had begun to fall apart. His dad had shown him how to use a map and compass and work out where he was on the mountain using latitude and longitude coordinates.

'This could be useful to you one day,' his dad had said. 'It could save your life.'

'Why can't we just use GPS?' Sam had asked him. Sam knew that the global positioning system could tell you your position using a car 'satnav' or handheld device.

'You could,' his dad had said, 'but being able to do it with a map and compass was always useful because they don't need batteries or recharging.' Sam had remembered that.

By now it was nearly lunchtime, so Ben, Zoe and Sam made their way back up through the village to the Edelweiss Restaurant. It was still quite early and Zoe's mum found them a table in the corner. She handed them the lunch menu.

'This can be my treat,' she said, 'seeing as it's the start of the holidays.' She left them to choose and went to attend to some other customers. In the end they decided to order a giant pizza to share, fries, a side salad each and drinks all round. One of the waiters came and took their order and left them to chat. Outside the restaurant window some children were sledging on the hillside. They each had a brightly coloured plastic tray and they were having races down the slope. It looked like fun.

'So, where shall we go tomorrow?' said Ben. Zoe unfolded the map they had each been given with their lift passes and spread it out on the table so they could all see.

'I think we should get as high as we can to get away from all the lift queues,' she said. 'If we take the Central lift up to Sugar Bowl, we can then ride the Express Chair up to Crystal Rock. If we stay on the easy runs above the Ski School, we're going to get caught up in all the crowds.'

Sugar Bowl was a beginners' area where people met for ski school. A large section was fenced off for the Penguin Club. There was an inflatable obstacle course for the youngest skiers to learn in safety.

'Yes, let's go for the Express Chair,' said Sam. 'That'll get us away from the early morning crush.' The Express Chair was just as described; a giant eight-seater chairlift that could sweep you at high speed up the mountain to Crystal Rock.

'Okay,' said Ben, 'that's the plan. When we get there we can decide what to do next.'

Zoe folded away the map just as the food arrived. It looked delicious. The waiter placed the giant pizza in the centre of the table. It was already cut into neat segments for them to help themselves.

'And three side salads and fries,' he said placing each of the dishes carefully on the table, before pouring their chosen drinks. 'Enjoy your meal.'

'Thank you,' said Zoe. 'You know what, guys? We should have a name.'

'How about The Three Amigos?' said Ben.

'No,' said Zoe, 'that's already been taken.'

'I know,' said Sam. 'We could call ourselves The Three Amigo-Skigos.'

'No,' said Ben, 'that's too long.'

'I've got it,' said Zoe. 'We'll be The Three Skigos.'

'The Three Skigos!' they all chanted and, with that, they all fell about laughing.

That celebration lunch would be one of the best meals they had ever shared. They laughed and joked about all the great things they planned to do. Little could they have guessed, on that first day of the holidays, what adventures lay ahead.

CHAPTER 4

The morning after their lunch celebration, Ben woke early to the sound of his radio alarm.

'This is the early morning news,' said the radio announcer. Ben rolled out of bed and pulled on his dressing gown.

'An investigation has been launched into a freak accident at Forest Ridge Junior School earlier this week,' said the voice from the radio. Ben turned up the volume. Their school had made the local news.

The newsreader continued, 'There are no reports of any injuries, and local officials hope to have the school reopened in the next few weeks. Avalanche protection measures above Forest Ridge are being reviewed and residents have been assured all essential safety work will be undertaken.'

Just as Ben was getting interested they moved on to another story. Why had no-one in their class been interviewed? It was their classroom that had been hit after all. It wasn't every day that an avalanche closes a school.

'And now we have the weather forecast for the local ski area.'

Ben pricked up his ears. 'Today it will be cloudy with sunny spells. Tomorrow it will be dry and sunny but further snow falls are expected by the end of the week. That's the early morning news. Now back to …' Ben switched off the radio.

There was so much to do and no time to lose. After he had showered, Ben looked out everything he needed for the day ahead. A day on the mountain meant you had to prepare well as you never knew how the weather might change. Being caught high on the mountain, in a blizzard and freezing temperatures, was a serious business. You could always take off some layers of clothing if you were too warm but you couldn't put them on if you'd left them behind. That's a lesson he'd learned from his dad quite early on.

He applied some high-factor sun cream to his face and neck, and put the rest of the tube in the side pocket of his backpack, along with some lip balm. The ultraviolet rays were strong at altitude, and there was no point in getting sunburned on the first day. After he had pulled on his thermals, ski socks and fleece, he took his ski jacket and trousers out of the wardrobe. Fortunately, they still fitted him from last year. Just to be safe, he slipped an extra fleece and some chocolate into his backpack, along with a pair of sunglasses.

The racing helmet he got for his last birthday was kept on display beside his bed. It was bright red with yellow and white markings. Ben carefully clipped on his ski goggles so that he wouldn't forget them and checked one last time that he had his lift pass, tissues and spending money. He was almost ready. Oh no, he'd forgotten his gloves. You wouldn't last five minutes on the mountain without warm gloves. He even squished a spare pair into his backpack just to be on the safe side. It was time for breakfast.

No-one was up yet so Ben helped himself to some cereal, toast and milk. His mum must have heard him moving about and came downstairs in her dressing gown.

'Well, you're up bright and early. Could that be because there's no school today?'

'I said I would meet Sam and Zoe up at the Edelweiss Restaurant at nine o'clock.'

His mum pushed back her hair. 'That's just as well because I can't afford to take any more time off work.' Ben's mum worked part-time at the local Medical Centre. 'I'm going to have to take Becky with me today whilst I arrange childcare.'

'You could always book her into the holiday ski club,' said Ben. 'They're meant to be starting up tomorrow.'

Ben's mum seemed interested. 'That's a good idea. I'll give them a ring.'

'What's a good idea?' said Becky as she came into the kitchen.

'You'll have to come to work with me today, Becky, but Ben has suggested you might like to join the holiday ski club. You'd like that.'

'Why can't I go with Ben?' Ben pretended not to hear.

'You're not old enough to go with Ben and his friends.'

'Yes I am,' said Becky. 'I'm almost nine.'

'You wouldn't be able to keep up with them.'

'Yes I would.'

'No, I'm sorry, Becky. Today you're coming with me and tomorrow we'll see about booking you into the holiday club. You'll have a great time.' Becky sat down at the kitchen table in a mood. She didn't like it when she didn't get her own way. She wasn't a baby.

'Now, Ben, could you make up your own packed lunch today. You'll find everything you need over there and in the fridge. I've got to see to Becky and get ready for work.' After he had finished his breakfast, Ben made up his sandwiches and found a piece of fruit, a couple of cereal bars and a fruit smoothie. Becky watched him from the kitchen table, still clearly not happy that she was missing out on all the fun. When he had finished, he found room for his packed lunch in his backpack.

'Bye, Becky, have a nice day.' Becky said nothing. Ben kept his ski boots in the utility room where they could dry out at the end of the day. He sat down on a bench and began to squeeze each foot into a boot before tightening the clasps. He pulled down the cuffs of his ski trousers, picked up his backpack and hobbled out of the back door to the garage.

His dad had left his skis and poles ready for him to collect. He had waxed and prepared the soles of the skis for Ben the night before, and the edges were sharp and glistening. Outside, Ben put on his safety helmet, gloves and backpack, and swung his skis up over his shoulder.

The bus journey up through the village didn't take long. From the bus terminus it was a short walk to the main lift station. His dad would have called it a good warm-up exercise. Zoe was already waiting at the Edelweiss Restaurant when he got there as her mum had to start work early. She was proud to show off the ski suit her mum had bought her for the new season. Five minutes later, Sam arrived, all kitted up. It was still quite early but they were eager and ready for the off.

Inside the main lift station, Forest Ridge Central, they had to climb a set of stairs to reach the ticket gates. The detector bleeped as it automatically read their lift passes and let them push through the turnstiles. The lift gondolas were moving slowly through the station, filling up with the first passengers of the day. As the doors of the next gondola to arrive swung open, Ben, Zoe and Sam piled on board and propped their skis against the window bar. Then, as they approached the exit, the doors slowly closed and the lift mechanism clamped the gondola tightly onto the moving cable. In an instant, they were out and climbing rapidly, leaving the lift station behind.

'Look down there,' said Sam. Two snowboarders were carving down the slope beneath them, leaving a long, snaking pattern in the snow.

'I'd like to try boarding some day just to see what it's like,' said Ben.

'I don't know,' said Zoe. 'It's harder than it looks and it really hurts when you fall.'

The gondola continued climbing, rocking and rumbling as it crossed over each support pylon. The slope below was steeper now, broken up by jagged black rocks. Their ears began to pop as the air pressure changed and the wind outside began to whistle. Soon the top station came into sight. They were almost there.

As the gondola swept into the Sugar Bowl lift station, it disengaged from the cable and ran onto the guide rail. Everyone got ready to leave. The doors swung open and they all piled out onto the rubber matting and made for the exit. Outside they had their first view of Sugar Bowl in almost a year, its gentle slopes waiting to welcome all those beginners who were trying skiing for the first time.

Ben dropped his skis onto the ground and cleaned the snow from the soles of his boots. He carefully stepped into each binding and clamped them closed. When they were all ready, they pushed off past the ski school and down towards the start of the Express Chair. The early morning ice rattled and scraped against the edges of their skis, singing like a well known song. At the entrance to the chair, they all braked sharply and funneled through the turnstiles, each choosing a separate lane and waiting their turn at the stop sign. As the barriers swung open, they slid through in a line and waited for the next chair to arrive. In an instant it was upon them. Sitting back, they were gathered up by the chair and swept off the ground. Ben stretched up and gently lowered the safety bar. They were on their way to Crystal Rock, high up on the mountain.

As they neared the top, Zoe lifted the safety bar. The moment their skis touched the snow, they all pushed forward and glided down the exit ramp, coming gently to rest beside the direction signpost in front of the Crystal Rock Restaurant.

'Right,' said Ben, 'what's the plan?' There were three possible runs they could take from this point. An easy run called Everglade, an intermediate one called Bluebell and a difficult run called Challenge.

'I think we should go for the easy one first,' said Zoe. 'There's no point in getting injured before we're properly warmed up.'

'I'll go with that,' said Sam.

'Okay,' said Ben, 'Everglade it is.' He adjusted his goggles and tapped his ski poles together. 'Is everyone ready? Then, let's go.'

Ben pushed off in a long glide, with Zoe following close behind and Sam taking up the rear. A thin layer of powder snow covered the firm base beneath, which made for great skiing. As the slope steepened, Ben threw in a couple of narrow turns to control his speed and Zoe and Sam followed in his tracks. Ahead of them was a group of slower skiers. Ben planted his ski pole and swung left to avoid the group, the edge of his ski carving into the snow. Zoe chose to go right, followed closely by Sam. Now they were really flying and with the way ahead clear, Sam went into a tuck, streamlining his body as his skis accelerated across the snow.

In an instant he had overtaken Zoe and was catching Ben, sitting back on the tails of his skis to gain speed. Suddenly, Sam spotted a jump, a mound of snow at the side of the run. Standing up, he edged sharply to turn across the slope and line himself up with the ramp. As he hit the mound, the tips of his skis were launched upward and he flew through the air. A sudden gust of wind threatened to knock him backwards and he had to compensate by cycling his arms forwards to keep his balance. He hit the snow with a loud thud and flexed his knees to absorb the impact. Luckily, he just managed to hold it together. As he regained control, Zoe came flying past. She overtook him with a whoop of delight, but the sound of her voice was snatched away by the wind. This was the excitement of skiing they had waited for all year.

Ben knew they were now approaching a junction where two runs crossed. Standing up tall to kill some of his speed, he swung in a wide turn to the side of the run. Digging in his edges, he braked sharply and shuddered to a rapid stop. Zoe spotted his move and swept around behind him, stopping safely downhill. They were both out of breath, gasping in the thin mountain air. Sam was not far behind. After a couple of braking turns, he glided in to join them, the edge of his ski throwing up a spray of ice crystals.

'Oh, that was great,' said Sam. 'Did you see my jump?'

'Yes,' said Zoe, 'I thought you were going to wipe out.'

'You couldn't ask for better conditions,' said Ben. 'This snow is perfect.'

Once they had all regained their breath, Zoe took a turn to lead off. Far below they could see the drag lift that would take them back to the top. Sam followed her and, this time, Ben stayed at the back. When they reached the drag lift, there was only a small queue. Zoe grabbed hold of the tow bar, kicked through the release wand and shot off up the tow track. One by one, they were whisked back up the mountain to Crystal Rock.

They spent the rest of the morning on the intermediate run called Bluebell. Although more difficult than Everglade, the Bluebell run held no fears. In places the slope dropped away suddenly and they had to dig in their edges to control their speed but it was still quite an easy run. Alongside Bluebell, the Snowcat machines had carved out a Ski Cross racecourse with rollers, dips, twists and turns. Ben, Zoe and Sam tried it out, racing one another down the track, almost knocking each other over in their excitement. It was great fun even if they wouldn't have won any real competitions.

Half way down there was a small café, perched on a rocky ledge overlooking the valley. They stopped there for their mid-morning break, to warm themselves up with a hot chocolate. There was a log fire burning in the corner, and on the walls were old pictures of Forest Ridge before it became a ski resort. It was very cosy, and just the place to take shelter if the weather turned bad.

A chairlift took them back up the mountain to Crystal Rock. By lunchtime they were really hungry, and as they had each brought a picnic they found a sheltered spot outside in the sun and sat down to enjoy their lunch. Somehow, food always seems to taste better when you're up on the mountain in the fresh air.

When they had cleared up, they trudged over to the Crystal Rock Restaurant to buy some hot drinks. There was a self-service section, with outside seating on a wooden terrace that gave a great view of all the surrounding peaks. High above, and to the right, was Eagle Summit and over to the left they could just make out the Glacier Station high above Silver Lake. To reach Eagle Summit you had to take the cable car from Crystal Rock but it could only run if the wind was not too strong.

Zoe unfolded her map and checked on the difficult run they had not yet tried. It ran all the way from Crystal Rock back down to Sugar Bowl.

'Who wants to try the Challenge run after lunch?' she said. Ben was keen.

'Yes, let's risk it. It's not that difficult. We managed it last year.'

'I'm up for it,' said Sam. 'I fancy a challenge.'

As they were reapplying sun cream and getting their things together Ben suddenly recognised someone he wasn't expecting. Coming across the terrace, with a tray of drinks, was Marcus. He was with a girl they had never seen before.

'Marcus,' Ben called out. Marcus spotted them and came across to the next table.

'Hi there,' said Marcus. 'Fancy meeting you here.' Ben was puzzled.

'Is your school closed as well, Marcus?' Marcus seemed a little embarrassed.

'Well, not exactly. It's the last week and there's not much going on so we decided to slip away early. No-one will notice. Sorry, have you met Carla? She's in the same year as me.'

Carla was wearing a silver, designer ski jacket with a white, furry collar. Zoe noticed her nails were carefully manicured, and painted, and she was listening to background music on one of the latest phones. She wouldn't have looked out of place on a catwalk.

'Hi, Carla, I'm Zoe. This is Ben and Sam. We're in the same class.'

Carla smiled. 'Oh, you're still in junior school then? We've left all that behind, haven't we, Marcus?' Marcus looked uncomfortable.

'Look,' said Marcus, 'you won't tell anyone about seeing us here, will you?'

'Why should we?' said Ben. 'It's none of our business.' Marcus seemed relieved. He sat down and pulled his chair closer.

'Listen, remember what we talked about last summer?'

'What?' said Zoe. 'You mean about skiing over to Silver Lake?'

Marcus hesitated. 'Yes, Carla and I are planning to do it tomorrow. The weather forecast is good and we want to take the chance whilst we can.' Ben and Sam looked at one another but said nothing.

Zoe was more forthright. 'You can't be serious. You can't take the risk.'

Carla replied abruptly. 'Of course we can, Marcus. Don't listen to her. You're a great skier. You told me yourself.'

'Look, forget about it,' said Marcus. 'If you don't want to join us, that's up to you. Just don't tell anyone.' Marcus and Carla finished their drinks and stood up to leave.

'How long do you think it will take?' asked Ben.

'No more than two hours,' said Marcus. 'We'll be there and back by lunchtime.'

'We'll tell you all about our adventure when we get back,' said Carla.

'Be seeing you,' said Marcus. And with that they walked away. For a moment, no-one spoke. No-one seemed to know what to say. Then Ben broke the silence.

'Do you think they're serious?'

'I think they're serious,' replied Sam.

'Well, actually,' said Zoe, 'I don't think they're serious. I think they're stupid.'

Although they didn't realise it at the time, meeting Marcus and Carla on that fateful day would change all their lives.

CHAPTER 5

With lunch over Ben, Zoe and Sam had other things on their minds. They still had to take on the difficult run called Challenge.

Gathering their skis and poles from the rack beside the Crystal Rock Restaurant, they snapped their ski boots into their bindings. It was now two o'clock and the sun had started to soften the snow. Lower down the mountain it would be heavy and turning to slush.

'It's over this way,' said Sam pointing in the direction of the signpost. Zoe and Ben followed him, gathering themselves for what lay ahead. At first the run was gentle and strangely deceptive, but they knew, from past experience, what to expect. Before long they came upon a sharp turn that gave no warning of what was to come. The only clue was a small group of wary skiers standing on the edge, looking down, and trying to find the courage to take the next step.

When Sam, Zoe and Ben reached this spot, they stopped to gather their thoughts. Looking down, the slope dropped steeply away. In front of them lay a long, sheer ribbon of snow carved by skiers into a quilt of mounds, bumps, hollows and troughs. This was a bump slope, a mogul field, and their next challenge.

Sam was the first to take the plunge. Pushing forward, he dropped off the ledge and onto the slope, edging his right ski to start his first turn. Riding up and over the first bump, he turned on the crest and slid down the other side, braking as he went. Rebounding upwards, he mounted the next mogul, turning in the opposite direction, before sinking down in preparation for the next mound. He was into a rhythm now and descending at speed.

Zoe followed Sam but chose a route down the side of the run, rising and falling over the bumps, fighting to control her speed and direction and, hopefully, avoid a crunching tumble. Ben was not far behind. Seeing a gap in front of him, he dropped over the edge and gave pursuit, his eyes fixed on the next turn in his path, his brain concentrating hard and planning the best, and safest, route down the steep, rutted slope. It was exhilarating and it was terrifying, but it was fun.

Suddenly it happened. Sam was travelling at speed when the inside edge of his ski clipped a frozen ball of ice or, as Ben would call it, a crunch cookie. In an instant, his ski was deflected upwards and outwards, spinning him around with no chance to recover. As if in slow motion he took to the air, out of control and with no way back. Knowing what was going to happen next, he pulled in his arms, tried to relax and waited.

As he hit the snow, his helmet and head flew backwards and he instinctively closed his eyes. The thud when it came knocked the wind out of him and he rolled into a ball. Luckily, his bindings broke instantly and his skis flew off in different directions. Tumbling down the hard slope, his ski poles were wrenched from his grip before he continued in a long slide down the icy surface. Eventually, after what seemed an age, he came to a halt.

When he opened his eyes, all he could see was white. His goggles had filled up with snow. Carefully, he moved his feet and then his arms, before rolling over onto his back. He still seemed to be in one piece and, fortunately, there didn't seem to be anything broken, apart from his pride. As he sat up, Zoe appeared by his side.

'Now that's what I call a fall,' said Zoe, trying to stay calm. 'How do you feel?'

'No problem,' said Sam. 'It was just a little tumble.'

Zoe had collected Sam's ski poles on the way down. He had slid a long way. She handed him his poles to help him get up. In a moment, Ben appeared carrying Sam's skis. He tried to sound casual.

'I'm sorry, Sam. I didn't quite have time to get my camera out. Could you do that fall again so that I can get a photo?' Sam laughed and got to his feet. He would probably have quite a few bruises tomorrow but, fortunately, there was no real harm done.

When Sam had cleaned off the soles of his boots, he reset his bindings and clamped himself back into his skis. Zoe cleaned and dried his ski goggles for him and Ben helped to clip them back onto his safety helmet. After what had happened, they decided to take the rest of the run at a more leisurely pace.

As they made their way down the mountain, they had time to reflect on how things can suddenly go wrong when you least expect it. By the time they reached Sugar Bowl, it was well after three o'clock so they decided to call it a day. From Sugar Bowl they followed the snow covered road as it twisted and turned, down through the trees, towards the lift station at Forest Ridge Central. By the time they got back to the Edelweiss Restaurant, it was almost four o'clock, around the time when they would usually be finishing school. Inside, Zoe's mum was already clearing up for the day.

'Hello, Zoe, did you have a nice day?'

'Great,' said Zoe. 'Sam had a spectacular fall.' Her mum seemed concerned.

'Oh no, nothing serious I hope?'

'No problem, Mrs Roberts,' said Sam. 'It was just a little tumble.'

'Everyone knows Sam is made of rubber,' said Ben. 'He bends easily but he doesn't break.' And they all laughed at that, even Zoe's mum.

'I'll tell you what. We've got some fresh cream gateaux left over that's just going to go to waste. Would you like some?'

'Yes, please,' they all chorused.

'Well, why don't you take a seat over there in the corner and I'll go and get it.'

While they were waiting, Ben suddenly remembered about Marcus and Carla. They'd been so busy getting down Challenge, he'd forgotten all about them.

'Do you think Marcus and Carla will be alright?'

'What could go wrong?' said Sam. 'They said it would only take them two hours.'

'Yes,' said Ben, 'but what if they don't make it? No-one will know if they don't reach Silver Lake safely.'

'Ben's got a point,' said Zoe. 'We're the only ones who know what they're planning to do.' Everyone went quiet. Then, suddenly, Ben had an idea.

'Why don't we go over to Silver Lake tomorrow to meet them? Then we'll know for sure that they've made it.' It suddenly seemed like a good idea. Zoe's mum came over with three plates of fresh cream gateaux. It looked scrumptious.

'Mum, we've just had an idea. Would it be alright if we took a bus to Silver Lake tomorrow? They say the skiing there is great.' Zoe's mum thought for a moment.

'I don't see why not,' she said, 'but, of course, Ben and Sam will have to check first with their parents to see if they agree.' She left them to enjoy the gateaux.

'Okay,' said Ben, 'that's the plan. If everyone agrees, we'll meet here tomorrow and catch the morning bus to Silver Lake. Remember to bring lots of supplies. It could be a long day.'

When they had finished eating, they shook hands on it and headed off home. Ben's dad had finished early and was sitting in the kitchen, drinking coffee and reading his newspaper, when Ben got in.

'So, what sort of day did you have, Ben?' said his dad as Ben sat down at the table.

'We had a great time,' said Ben. 'Sam had a wipeout but he's okay.'

'Well,' said his dad, 'as long as you stick to the patrolled slopes, you can always get help if you need it.' Ben went very quiet and then plucked up his courage.

'Dad?'

'Yes?' Ben's dad looked up from his newspaper.

'Zoe, Sam and I were thinking of taking the bus over to Silver Lake tomorrow. Is that okay?' Ben held his breath.

'Oh, I don't see why not,' said his dad. 'They say the snow is really good over there.' Ben was relieved. His mum who was listening turned around.

'Oh, wait a minute. I was hoping Ben could take Becky up to the holiday ski club at Sugar Bowl tomorrow. I need to get to work.' Fortunately, Ben's dad came to the rescue.

'That shouldn't be a problem. Ben can drop Becky off at Sugar Bowl and still be in time. The bus to Silver Lake doesn't leave till ten o'clock. There's a bus back at lunchtime and another one at four o'clock.' Ben's mum still seemed unsure.

'Well, as long as the three of them stay together, Steve. We don't want to have to send out a search party.' Ben's dad went back to reading his newspaper.

'Don't worry, Sue, they'll be fine. They need to learn to take responsibility for themselves.' And, with that, it was decided.

That evening Ben looked out all the things he thought he would need for the day's adventure to Silver Lake. He put a torch, a compass and some extra chocolate into his backpack. Then he had an idea. Last winter his dad had bought him a small emergency tent to play with in the snow. It didn't have any tent poles or pegs. It was just for sheltering on the mountain if you got caught in a blizzard. His dad had shown him how to use it one day, just for fun. Ben found the bright orange tent, stored in a nylon bag, hanging on a hook in the garage. It was extra lightweight so Ben was able to stuff it into his backpack, without too much trouble. It would be a good chance to try it out again.

When it was time for bed, Ben went upstairs to his room with a mug of hot milk. He wanted to get a good night's sleep. In the light of his bedside lamp, he opened the book he was reading. It was an adventure about a group of school children who go off on a trip. Their bus breaks down on a high mountain pass and they are stranded. Ben was beginning to feel sleepy.

He had just got to the part where the driver of the bus goes to try to get help, and the children are left all alone with their teacher. Then one of the children notices that one of their classmates is missing. They have left the bus. What are they going to do? Ben never got any further that night. He fell asleep propped up on his pillow, with the book lying open on his chest.

Later on, his mum looked in before retiring for the night. She put the book away, eased the pillow from under his head and pulled up the covers. Picking up the empty mug, she switched off the bedside light and softly closed the bedroom door. Ben had a big day ahead of him.

CHAPTER 6

'But why do I have to go to the holiday club?' said Becky. 'Why can't I go to Silver Lake with Ben?'

'I've already explained.' Becky's mum was beginning to lose patience. 'You're not old enough. You wouldn't be able to keep up. Now, please don't ask me again.'

'Come on, Becky,' said Ben. 'We've got to go now or I'm going to miss the bus.' Becky reluctantly followed Ben to the back door. Max who was sitting there watching them, started to whine.

'Out of the way, Max,' said Ben. 'I haven't got time to play with you.' Max suddenly jumped up, putting his great paws on Ben's chest as if he didn't want him to leave. He seemed to be trying to tell him something. 'Oh, Max, you silly dog, you're keeping me back. I'll play with you when I get home tonight.' Ben pushed through the door, trailing Becky behind him. Max watched him go with a disappointed look in his eyes.

It was eight forty five by the time they met Zoe and Sam. Ben explained about having to take Becky up to Sugar Bowl for the holiday club.

'That's not a problem,' said Zoe. 'There's plenty of time. We'll go together. Here, Becky, you can take my hand.'

By the time they got to Sugar Bowl, a small queue was gathering outside the Ski School where the club was based.

'Excuse me,' said Ben, 'is this the queue for the holiday ski club?'

'Yes,' said a girl with a clipboard, 'if you just wait inside, we'll get you all sorted out once the others arrive.' Ben took Becky inside and found her a seat beside the wall. He checked his watch.

'Right, Becky, I'm going to have to go now. Trust me, you'll love it.' Ben left his little sister sitting there and went to rejoin Sam and Zoe who were waiting patiently outside. Becky was still clearly not happy but Ben couldn't help that.

As they made their way across to the lift to take the journey back down to the village, a strange thing happened. Who should they meet leaving the lift station but Marcus and Carla.

'So, you've changed your mind then?' said Marcus.

'What do you mean?' said Ben. Marcus seemed pleased.

'Have you decided to come with us after all?' Ben tried to explain but Zoe jumped in.

'We're going across to Silver Lake by bus. We'll meet you when you get there. Then we'll know you've made it safely.'

'Oh, I see,' said Marcus. He seemed disappointed. Carla said nothing.

'Look,' said Marcus, 'why don't you come with us to the top to see us off and wish us good luck? You'll still have time to catch the bus.' Ben, Sam and Zoe looked at each other. They'd known Marcus a long time so perhaps they owed him this.

'Okay,' said Zoe, 'we'll see you off, but remember, we don't want any part of this.'

Together, they clamped on their skis and made their way down to the Express Chair. It was still quiet so they were quickly on their way up the mountain. The weather forecast had been right. The sky was a deep blue as far as they could see and the sun felt warm on their faces. It was going to be a glorious day.

As they reached Crystal Rock, they slid off down the exit ramp and headed over towards the Eagle Summit cable car station. High above them they could see one cable car climbing as the other was descending. They were suspended from two, steel support ropes, with one cable car counter-balancing the other. It looked precarious but the aerial tramway was really quite safe. When they reached the lower cable car station, they all took off their skis and carried them up the steps to the waiting area. As the cable car arrived, it slowed to a snail's pace and slid into the loading bay. When it was secured and the brake applied, the doors slid open and they climbed inside. It was quite a crush as the compartment filled up with skiers. As he waited, Ben had a strange feeling that they were being followed.

'Sam,' said Ben, 'have you noticed any of the Ski Patrol around?'

'No,' said Sam, 'why do you ask?'

'I don't know,' said Ben. 'I just get the strange feeling we're being followed.' Zoe had overheard them talking.

'That's because you have a guilty conscience,' said Zoe in a whisper. 'You know what Marcus and Carla are planning to do and you're scared they are going to get caught by the Ski Patrol.' Ben thought Zoe could be right but he said nothing.

When they reached the top station they all piled out. The temperature was a lot cooler up there and the air thinner. Just walking seemed to take more effort. Marcus and Carla clamped themselves into their skis as Ben, Zoe and Sam watched on. There was quite a crowd around about them, eager to set off on the Cliffhanger run down to the resort of Timbermill. The village of Timbermill was some distance from Forest Ridge and in the opposite direction from Silver Lake.

'Okay,' said Ben, 'we had better get back on the cable car for the journey back down to Crystal Rock. All going well, we'll see you in Silver Lake in about two hours.'

That's when they received a bit of a shock. One of the cable car operators came out of the control room and closed off the entry gates.

'Excuse me,' said Zoe, 'we were planning to take the cable car back down.' The cable car operator was apologetic.

'Sorry, we've got a fault on the control panel. The cable car isn't going anywhere until we get the problem sorted out. You'll have to ski down the Cliffhanger run to Timbermill with all the others.'

The children looked at each other. The only direct run back down to Crystal Rock and Forest Ridge was the expert run called Precipice. Even if they had wanted to risk it, they couldn't because Precipice was closed due to avalanche danger. It was roped off and barred to even expert skiers. The Ski Patrol would be onto them in no time if they tried to go anywhere near it and they would all have their lift passes confiscated.

'It looks like you're going to have to come with us after all,' said Marcus. 'It will be safer if we all stick together.' Ben, Zoe and Sam could see they had a problem. How were they going to explain ending up in Timbermill, far from Forest Ridge or Silver Lake? They didn't even know if they would be able to get a bus back from there. How had they managed to get into this mess?

'Well, look,' said Carla, 'are you going to make up your mind or not? We haven't got all day.' Zoe felt like telling Carla exactly what she thought but she knew it would only make things worse. Reluctantly, Ben, Zoe and Sam clamped on their skis.

'Right,' said Marcus, 'stay close behind me so that you don't miss the way and keep your eyes open for the Ski Patrol.' The crowds at the top of Eagle Summit were beginning to thin out now. Marcus led them around, and down under the lift cable as if to take the Cliffhanger run to Timbermill. When they were out of sight of the cable car operators, he stopped at the side of the run. The last few stragglers skied past but he waited just to make sure no-one else was following them.

'Okay,' said Marcus, 'that seems to be the last of them. Follow me.' With that, Marcus lifted up the chequered tape that marked the edge of the run and slipped underneath. The others followed, one by one, each fearing that at any moment they would be spotted. Sliding down the slope behind the cable car station, they headed in the direction of Silver Lake. Although the snow was deep and ungroomed, it was skiable. Marcus stopped for a moment to let everyone catch up and to check that they were not being followed. They were now, well and truly, out of bounds.

'Right,' said Marcus, 'follow my tracks and stay close. We're in this together now.' No-one spoke. They skied in silence down the gentle slope which ran across the base of the glacier. After about fifteen minutes, Marcus brought them all to a halt.

'This is where we have to start turning down into Shepherds' Gully,' he explained. 'If we follow it downhill, it will eventually lead us to the ski runs above Silver Lake.' As they rested on their ski poles, they could hear the gentle gurgle of a nearby stream buried just beneath the snow. It was so quiet, so peaceful. And then, suddenly, Ben heard it. It was very faint at first, but it still startled him.

'Wait, wait, wait for me!' Everyone froze. Where had that come from?

'Quick, everyone,' shouted Marcus, 'get down.' As one, they all crouched against the slope and listened intently. Then, it came again.

'Please, please, wait for me!' In that awful moment, Ben recognised the voice and he suddenly knew why he had thought someone was following them.

Over the ridge, there appeared a figure, coming towards them and following in their tracks. The person was waving their arms in the air for attention but it was not one of the Ski Patrol. They were far too small for that.

'Oh no,' said Ben. 'Becky, what have you done?' At first, the others were relieved but then the full scale of what was happening began to sink in. Becky must have followed them all the way from Sugar Bowl up to Crystal Rock. Then she would have been in the cable car with them on the way up to Eagle Summit. That's why Ben had felt he was being followed. Becky must have seen them drop under the chequered tape when they left the Cliffhanger run, and followed their tracks in the fresh unbroken snow. Now she had managed to catch them up.

Becky slid down the last section of slope towards them, and fell, gasping and sobbing, in a crumpled heap at their feet.

'Becky,' said Ben, 'you silly, silly girl. You're supposed to be safe in the holiday club. Anything could have happened to you.' Ben was shaking as he spoke but it was not really from anger, it was from fear.

'Alright,' said Zoe. 'What's happened has happened. We can't change it now. At least we're all together.' Zoe slid across and pulled Becky to her feet. 'Okay, Becky, I want you to stop crying, right now. You wanted to come with us and now you're here, so stop making a fuss.' This direct approach seemed to do the trick. Becky stopped crying and wiped her eyes with her ski glove.

'Let's not hang about,' said Marcus. 'We're falling behind schedule.' He turned around and aimed his skis downhill. 'We'll just have to take it slowly. Everyone, try to stay together.'

Once more they set off, with Becky tucked in in front of Zoe, and with Ben taking up the rear. The journey, that was supposed to take just two hours, would now take much longer. However, if they could just stay calm, there was no reason why they could not make it safely down into Silver Lake. And that is what they did. An hour after they were supposed to reach their destination, Marcus, Carla, Ben, Zoe, Sam and Becky glided into Silver Lake, tired and exhausted.

Unfortunately, one thing was clear. They had missed the lunchtime bus back to Forest Ridge.

CHAPTER 7

'Well, what are we going to do now?' said Sam. 'There isn't another bus for ages.'

'I don't know about anyone else,' said Carla, 'but I need a drink. I'm parched.'

'There's a café over there,' said Marcus. 'Come on, I'll treat you all.' The children followed Marcus to a group of outside tables. They propped their skis against the wooden handrail and found themselves a seat.

'Oh, I would love a long cool drink,' said Sam, 'with plenty of ice.' A girl came out to take their order. Becky asked if she could have an ice-cream as well, seeing as Marcus was paying. She seemed to have recovered from her chase through the snow.

Silver Lake was a bit quieter than Forest Ridge, although still quite popular with skiers. In the summer there would be pleasure boats out on the lake, but at this time of year it was frozen over. When the ice was thick enough, they would sometimes mark out a circular track and hire out snowmobiles to holiday makers. You had to be careful though. One year there was a rapid thaw and one of the snowmobiles went straight through the ice. They had to fish it out, the next day, with a tractor.

When the cold drinks arrived, everyone was ready to quench their thirst. Marcus took out his wallet and paid the girl.

'So, what are we going to do then?' said Ben. 'We can't sit here for the rest of the day.' Marcus had taken out his map of the ski area and he was studying it carefully.

'Why don't we take a ride on the funicular?' said Marcus.

'What's a funicular?' asked Becky.

'It's a type of train,' explained Ben. 'It climbs up the mountain inside a tunnel, all the way up to the top of the glacier.' Marcus showed Becky the map.

'See, here it is,' said Marcus. 'This dotted line shows you where it goes, but of course you can't see it because it's inside the mountain. It climbs all the way up to Glacier Station, the very highest point you can reach.'

'And then what do we do?' asked Zoe. She couldn't help but feel this was another one of Marcus' plans.

'Then we ski all the way back down again, of course,' said Carla, 'in time to catch the bus home.' Zoe pulled the map towards her and studied it. She noticed that Marcus had marked the route they had followed this morning in red pen. There were other markings on the map as well.

'How difficult is the run?' said Zoe. 'I think we've had enough excitement for one day.'

'There are two runs down,' said Marcus, 'and one of them is marked intermediate so there shouldn't be a problem.'

'Sounds good to me,' said Ben. 'Let's give it a go.'

'Hold on, everyone,' said Carla. 'I want to get a photo.' Carla took out her expensive camera phone from an inside pocket and got them all to pose. 'Smile, everyone - one for the memory album - got it.'

When they had finished their drinks, they gathered up their skis and poles and headed for the entrance to the funicular railway. The train journey up to the top of the glacier was popular with walkers and sightseers, as well as skiers, so there was a queue waiting outside the station entrance. After a few minutes, the gates were unlocked and the crowd began to push forward; the turnstiles counted them through to ensure the train could not be overloaded. Everyone waited patiently in the entrance hall for the train to arrive. Behind them, the turnstiles had counted the maximum number of passengers allowed and locked automatically.

Suddenly, a horn sounded in the distance and two headlamps appeared in the mouth of the tunnel, the metal wheels braking and slowly creeping towards the buffers. The train had arrived. After the downhill passengers had left the train, the sliding doors opened and everyone began to surge forward. Ben held on tightly to Becky's hand. There was no way he was going to lose his little sister again. Inside the train, to allow for the steep slope of the tracks, the floor was set at an angle and in steps along the length of the carriage. When everyone was aboard a bell sounded, and slowly the train doors began to close. There was a slight shudder as the haul cable began to pull, and then they were off climbing rapidly, the wheels rattling beneath them. Through the windows they could see lights flashing by as the train climbed faster and faster, the wind whistling inside the tunnel.

'My ears hurt,' said Becky. Ben showed her how to hold her nose and blow to release the pressure. After what seemed like an age the train began to slow and there was light at the end of the tunnel. They had reached Glacier Station.

Outside, in the cold mountain air, they all gathered for some more photographs using Carla's phone. From the viewing platform you could see in every direction.

'Look,' said Sam, 'you can see Silver Lake down below. It looks tiny.'

'I can see Eagle Summit,' said Ben pointing into the distance. 'Just think that's where we were this morning.'

Eagle Summit was lower than Glacier Station, with the long slope of the glacier in between. But Ben knew that, beautiful though it looked, the glacier held hidden dangers. Anywhere beneath the frozen snow there could be deadly cracks in the rock, or huge deep crevasses waiting to catch out any careless walker or skier. Only expert mountaineers would dare to cross it, and only then roped together with ice axes at the ready.

'I don't like the look of that sky,' said Zoe. Everyone followed her view. Over to the west, heavy clouds were beginning to move in. The weather was changing. 'It's just as well we'll miss the worst of it,' she said.

'Yes,' said Ben, 'more snow is forecast in the next few days.'

'Okay,' said Marcus, 'I think we've seen enough. It's time to get going.'

Everyone collected their skis and carried them down the metal grid steps to the snow below and prepared to set off. The wind had started to get up and it was feeling decidedly chilly at the top of the mountain. Marcus had checked the map one more time and he seemed to know where he was going. When they were all ready, he headed off down the intermediate run, as planned, which seemed easy enough. When they reached a junction where the run split in two, he stopped to give everyone time to catch up.

'I think we go left now,' said Marcus.

'You think?' said Zoe. 'You mean you don't know? I think we'd better check the map again.'

'No, there's no need,' said Marcus. 'This is the way we have to go. Follow me, everyone.' Marcus led off and everyone followed behind, eager to get back down the mountain. After a few minutes, the slope became steeper and the snow deeper. Ben had noticed that there were no longer any ski tracks ahead of them but Marcus seemed to know what he was doing. Eventually, with the snow becoming heavier, they were forced to push forward with their ski poles just to keep going. Suddenly, Marcus halted and got out his ski map. He appeared to have a puzzled look on his face.

'What's the problem?' asked Carla.

'There's nothing to worry about,' said Marcus. 'I think we may have taken a wrong turning.'

'A wrong turning?' said Zoe. 'You mean we're lost?'

'It's not a problem,' said Marcus. 'I know where we are.'

'The problem is we shouldn't be here,' said Zoe. 'We're out of bounds - again.'

'Look, I know what I'm doing,' said Marcus. 'There's no point in going back now. It's too far to climb back up. We'll have to go forward.'

'Forward to where?' asked Ben.

'Down across the glacier,' said Marcus, pointing in the direction of Eagle Summit far below them.

'You can't be serious,' said Zoe. 'The glacier is dangerous.' Marcus looked straight at her.

'I'm afraid we have no choice. There's no other way out of here.' Everyone stood in silence, trying to take in what Marcus had just said. Marcus put away the map and pushed forward with his ski poles. No-one said anything. They just fell in behind him in a long silent column, heading down across the glacier in the direction of Eagle Summit.

The first flakes of snow had started to fall but they had no choice but to keep moving forward. Ben's brain was now in a daze. How had they managed to get themselves into this awful mess? The sky was darker now and the snow was falling more heavily. Slowly the sun passed behind a bank of cloud and the wind picked up, whipping the snow into their faces, stinging their cheeks with ice crystals. They plodded on, their heads down, pressing forward against the wind. Why hadn't they taken more notice of the weather forecast? How had they managed to make a mistake and take a wrong turning?

Soon they were in a howling blizzard and, even with ski goggles, they could hardly see more than a few metres in front them. In the end, they could no longer keep going and Marcus brought them all to a halt, beside a large rocky outcrop.

'I'm sorry,' he said, 'it's no use. We can't go on.'

One by one, they each sank down in the snow, shivering, exhausted and just wanting to rest. But Ben knew they couldn't give up now. They had to do something to get out of the storm.

Suddenly, he had an idea.

CHAPTER 8

Unclamping his bindings, Ben stepped out of his skis and drove his poles into the deep snow. Then, pulling off his backpack, he started to undo the fastenings.

'Sam,' he shouted above the roar of the wind, 'give me a hand.' Together, Ben and Sam used their gloved hands to dig out a hollow in the snow behind the rock, where there was some protection from the worst of the wind. Then, opening his backpack, Ben pulled out the nylon bag and started to unfold the emergency tent.

At first, it seemed as though the storm would wrench it from their hands but they held on for dear life and pinned it to the ground with their knees.

'Becky,' shouted Ben, 'we need your help.' Becky used her poles to unclip her skis and crawled over to her brother on all fours.

'Quick, Becky,' said Ben, 'it's time for a spot of camping. Climb inside and move up to the back. You can be our first tent pole.' When she was inside, Zoe and Carla crawled in after her. Marcus and Sam followed and then, lastly, Ben grabbed his backpack and squeezed inside, pulling the opening flap down and under him. At least, now, they had some shelter.

Everyone just sat there, worn out and drained of energy. The orange nylon fabric cast an eerie glow over their pale faces, whilst outside the wind tugged at the skin of the tent, threatening to whip it away with one strong gust. The storm battered and blew and flapped around them, as if angry at their presence on the mountain, but their little shelter held firm. For the moment, they were safe.

'We can't stay here for long,' said Sam.

'What are we going to do?' said Ben.

Sam struggled out of his backpack, took off his gloves and undid the fastenings. Delving inside, he found the new map he had bought that week. It was much more detailed than the ski map and showed the whole of the mountain area. Sam found Glacier Station and traced his finger across the map towards Eagle Summit.

'We're somewhere in between,' he said, 'but how far have we come?'

'I don't know,' said Marcus. 'It's difficult to tell.' His voice sounded weary.

'There's a refuge on the glacier,' said Sam, 'an old shepherd's hut that mountaineers use if they are in trouble. I passed it with my dad last summer. It should be marked on the map.' Sam pored over the area where he had walked with his dad, moving his finger systematically over the surface, searching for a sign.

'I've got it,' he shouted. 'Quick, someone, give me a pen.' Everyone searched in vain for something to write with.

'Here,' said Marcus, 'you can use this.' Marcus handed him a red, ball-point pen.

'Right,' said Sam as he circled the tiny shape on the map marked refuge. 'Now all we need to do is work out where we are now.' Zoe had an idea.

'We stopped beside a large rock. Is that marked on the map?' Sam shook his head.

'The glacier is covered with large rocks. Which one do we choose?' Carla took out her phone and switched it on. Maybe she could make a phone call. They all waited in hope.

'Any luck?' asked Ben. 'Can you get a signal?'

'It's searching for the network,' said Carla. Sam suddenly had an idea.

'Carla, does your phone have GPS?'

'I don't know,' she said. 'What's GPS?' Sam seemed excited about something.

'Does it use a global positioning system?'

'It's one of the latest,' said Marcus, 'so it probably does.'

'Let's hope it does,' said Sam. 'Any luck with the signal?'

'Yes,' said Carla. 'Yes, I think I've got it.'

'Good,' said Sam, 'then take my photo.'

'What?' said Carla puzzled.

'Please, Carla, just do as I say,' said Sam impatiently. 'I've just had an idea.' Carla held up the lens and snapped him. Sam took the camera phone off her and studied the screen. His hopes fell. 'It's no use,' he said. 'The GPS coordinates are not showing up on the photo. It must need a computer to display the information.'

Sam switched off the camera and went to hand the phone back to Carla. Then, suddenly, he stopped. A symbol on the phone's main screen had caught his eye. 'Unless,' he said, 'it has a built-in digital compass.' Everyone waited with bated breath. 'Yes!' he shouted. 'We're in luck. Quick, Carla, read out what is written at the bottom of the screen.'

'There are some numbers and a letter,' said Carla, 'and then some more numbers and another letter.' She read them out and Sam wrote them down on the edge of the map. He then took the phone from her and checked them carefully himself before handing it back.

'Oh no,' said Carla, 'now I've lost the signal.'

'Never mind,' said Ben. 'Switch it off to save power. We can try again later.'

Sam took a small plastic ruler from his backpack and measured carefully across and up the surface of the map. Everyone sat in silence, not wishing to disturb him. After a few minutes he spoke quietly, almost in a whisper.

'I think I know where we are,' he said, marking a tiny red cross on the map. 'We're here, just beside this rocky outcrop.'

'How do you know?' said Zoe.

'The phone helped us,' said Sam. 'It uses GPS to keep track of our exact location. The built-in digital compass gave us our position on the map, using latitude and longitude coordinates.'

'Yes, but what do we do now?' said Marcus. 'If we know where we are, how do we find our way to the refuge?' Sam was already at work. Taking his compass out of his backpack, he laid it on the map and aligned it with the direction arrows. He then rotated the map and compass until the red needle was pointing directly north.

'Now, all we need is a bearing,' said Sam. Placing the compass over their location on the map, he carefully rotated the compass arrow in the direction of the refuge.

All the others looked on, unsure but fascinated. 'There,' said Sam, 'if I just follow the arrow and keep the red needle pointing north, I should reach the refuge. It will be safer if I find it first and then come back to show you the way.'

'But what if you get lost?' said Zoe. 'How will you get back?' Sam had an idea.

'Becky,' said Sam, 'do you know those sweets you like - the ones with all different colours? Do you have any in your backpack?' Becky seemed surprised.

'You mean these ones?' She held up a large bag of multi-coloured sweets.

'Could I borrow them please so that I can find my way back?' said Sam. Becky handed over the bag of sweets, puzzled but wanting to help.

'Okay,' said Sam, pulling on his gloves and adjusting his goggles, 'I'll be back as soon as I can.' Grabbing the compass, he slipped out of the tent and disappeared. Ben checked his watch. Time was getting on. In another hour it would start to get dark and then what would they do? They all sat in silence not knowing what to say. After what seemed like ages, Ben checked his watch again. Half an hour had passed and there was still no sign of Sam.

Then, suddenly, there was a scuffling noise outside the tent and everyone sat bolt upright. Through the entrance flap crawled Sam, covered in snow from head to foot - a real life, abominable snowman. He was breathing heavily but just managed to get his words out.

'I've found it,' he said. 'Get your skis on and get ready to move.' Outside the tent, the bright light from the snow made them blink and pull down their goggles. Fortunately, the snow and wind had eased a little as they prepared to move off. Ahead of them lay a line of brightly coloured sweets, dropped at intervals by Sam. They were not yet covered by the snow. As they moved off in a line, a strong gust of wind caught their precious tent and sent it flying, like a kite, into the distance. There was no going back.

Sam led the way, his compass in his hand and, this time, Marcus brought up the rear. It was a struggle but they battled on, buoyed up by the thought that they were in reach of shelter. The line of sweets had disappeared now so they could only trust Sam's navigational skills and hope that he had not made an error. Then, just when doubts were beginning to enter their minds, a dark shape loomed up out of the blizzard. They had reached the refuge.

Unclipping his skis, Sam trudged around the back of the building, out of the wind, and found a heavy wooden door. Great drifts of snow were piled up against it.

'Come round here,' he shouted. 'I've found the way in.' Picking up their skis, they followed Sam's path and found him digging away at the snow with his hands. They all joined in to help. Ben chipped away at the ice around the door with a ski pole and Zoe worked to release the frozen bolt holding the door closed. If they couldn't get inside, all their efforts would be in vain. At last, the bolt began to shift and Zoe managed to slowly pull it back out of its socket. Using his shoulder, Ben was able to push the door back just enough to squeeze through. They were inside.

Winter light filtered through a small, frosted window revealing a tiny room with a stone floor. They got all their gear inside and pushed the door tight against the wind and snow. The refuge was basic to say the least but, at that moment, for all the children it was the best shelter in the world.

In the corner was an old wood burning stove and nearby was a small pile of logs. Sam got down on all fours to see how it worked. Inside were some cold embers, and there was a chimney pipe to carry smoke up and out through the roof. It had been used and, probably, not that long ago.

In another corner were a couple of wooden crates that someone may have used in the summer to bring up supplies, and there was a small cupboard built into the wall. Sam was already poking around, like a ferret, to see what he could discover.

'Look what I've found,' he said holding up a plastic bag tied with a knot. Inside was a piece of paper and what seemed to be a half empty, disposable lighter. He opened the bag, took out the piece of paper and read the note in the dim light.

'I leave this lighter to whoever finds it,' read Sam. 'It saved my life and I hope it saves yours.' Sam slipped the precious lighter into his pocket. 'Right,' he said, 'first we need some kindling.' He had spotted the two wooden crates. 'This will do.'

Together the children started to break up the wooden crates, stamping on them with their heavy ski boots. Soon they had a pile of thin, splintered wood which they laid beside the stove. Sam was now busy rooting amongst the stonework and roof supports for anything he could find that was dry and combustible. After a few minutes, he had gathered a small bundle of moss and dried grass which he placed neatly on the stone floor beside the stove. Carefully, he built a lattice of the thinnest pieces of wood and into the spaces he poked some of the moss and dried grass. All the children looked on, not sure what to expect. Then, at last, there came the moment of truth.

Taking out the disposable lighter, Sam struck it a few times. Nothing happened. He tried again, harder this time and then, suddenly, a small flicker of flame appeared. Putting the flame to the dried moss and grass, he waited for it to catch light. Then, bending down on his hands and knees, he blew gently as it smouldered away. Gradually a bit of blue appeared and then yellow. They had a fire.

Taking his time, Sam slowly added pieces of wood, allowing the flames to grow. They all looked on, mesmerised by the flames, hoping against hope that the fire would not go out. When he thought it was safe to do so, he gently placed a log on the fire and watched the flames crackle and leap around its surface. Turning around, with a look of relief on his face, he grinned at everyone.

'Success,' he said. 'We have a fire. We have heat.'

It was only then that the children realised that they hadn't eaten since morning. Their packed lunches were still in their backpacks. Sitting there in the failing light, they shared everything out, even the two flasks of coffee which were, by now, lukewarm. Once again, Sam came to the rescue. In the cupboard, he found an old camping tin, with a detachable handle. Pouring some of the coffee into the tin, he placed it on the top of the stove and, in a few minutes, it was simmering away. At least they could all share a hot drink. Even Becky played her part.

'Look,' she said, 'look what I've got.' She emptied out the contents of her backpack onto the stone floor. She had enough chocolate and sweets to keep them all going for some time. Only Ben sounded a note of caution.

'I think we should ration our supplies of food,' he said. 'We don't know how long it will have to last.'

'What do you mean?' said Carla. 'They're bound to come looking for us soon. They're sure to find us. If only I can get a signal on my phone.'

'Unfortunately,' said Ben, 'they may not even know we're missing yet and, as for finding us, how will they know where to look?'

CHAPTER 9

Outside the holiday ski club at Sugar Bowl, a small group was gathered. Steve Harper, a member of the Forest Ridge Ski Patrol, was trying to stay calm.

'Her name is Becky, Becky Harper. My son, Ben, brought her here this morning.' The girl from the holiday club was studying her clipboard, clearly anxious.

'Yes, we do have a Becky Harper booked in for today but she doesn't appear to have turned up. Are you sure there wasn't a change of plan?'

'No, she was definitely meant to be here today. My wife asked me to collect her. She would have called me if there had been a change of plan.'

'Perhaps she's still with your son. Have you checked?'

'No, I can't. He's with his friends in Silver Lake. Look, I had better make a call.' Steve Harper took out his phone and dialled home. After what seemed like an age, his wife answered. 'Hi, Sue, there's a bit of a problem. Do you, by any chance, have Becky with you?' There was a pause. 'No, I'm at the holiday club and she's not here.' There was another pause. 'I know but they say she never turned up. Is there any chance she may have gone with Ben to Silver Lake?' On the other end of the line, Sue Harper's voice was becoming agitated, so he tried to stay calm. 'Yes, I know what we agreed but you remember what she's like. What time does the last bus from Silver Lake get into Forest Ridge?' Steve Harper checked his watch. 'Look, don't worry. The chances are she'll be with Ben and the others. I'll get straight down to the bus station now and meet them. I'm sure it's just a mix up. I'll phone you as soon as I have news.'

The journey down the mountain from Sugar Bowl seemed to take longer than usual. Why would Ben take Becky to Silver Lake with him when she was booked into the holiday club? It just didn't make sense. When he got out of the Central lift station, he made straight for his car which he'd left in the staff car park. The predicted snow was now falling quite heavily, so he switched on his car headlights and pulled out onto the road. The main bus station was at the centre of the village, near the ice rink and leisure pool. He pulled into a parking bay and checked his watch again. The last bus from Silver Lake was due in the next few minutes. He tried to think what he was going to say to Ben and Becky when they got off the bus. He had better try to stay calm until he had a full explanation.

At that moment, the bus he was expecting swung around the bend at the bottom of the hill and started climbing towards him. It pulled up outside the bus station and the doors opened with a hiss of air. The passengers climbed down the steps, some with skis, others with shopping bags. They were mostly adults. He waited. There was no sign of Ben, Becky or the others. Quickly, he got out of his car and went across to the driver.

'I'm here to pick up some children,' he said. He described them as best he could.

'Sorry,' said the driver, 'I didn't pick up any children on their own in Silver Lake.' Steve Harper was now even more puzzled.

'Is this the last bus today from Silver Lake?'

'I'm afraid so,' said the driver. 'Sorry I can't be more helpful.' With a swish the doors closed and the bus pulled away.

'Where on earth are they?' he said to himself. 'Surely they can't have missed the bus in Silver Lake?' Steve Harper got out his phone. 'Listen, Sue, they're not on the bus. Could you get on the phone to Sam's dad and Zoe's mum and let them know the situation. They may have missed the bus so I'm going to drive over to Silver Lake to have a look for them. I'll get back to you as soon as I have more information.'

The road over to Silver Lake was quite difficult at the best of times. Today, in the heavy snow, it needed extra care. If they'd missed the bus in Silver Lake they would just have to stay put. Why, even at that moment, they were probably sitting in a café, looking for change to phone home. Kids don't half worry their parents at times.

By the time Steve Harper pulled into Silver Lake it was already dark. He drove twice up and down the main street. There was no sign of them. He parked up outside the bus terminus. Searching for them in the snow might take some time, so he pulled on a thick, hooded jacket. He started at one end of the village and worked his way systematically through all the places he thought they may be hanging out but, in the end, he drew a blank. They were just nowhere to be found. At that point, his phone rang and he answered it. It was his wife.

'No, I'm afraid not. I've had no luck. We're going to have to report them missing. We need extra help.' Steve Harper hung up and made a call to the emergency services. If the children were missing and they were not in Silver Lake that could mean they were still on the mountain. Even though the local ski patrol would have checked all the runs before closing down for the day, there was always the possibility that they had strayed from one of the main runs and been missed. Time was now of the essence.

Within an hour of his phone call, a large group of volunteers from the local search and rescue team had gathered outside the main lift station in Silver Lake. They were led by Rick Edwards and Kate Jensen from the Forest Ridge Ski Patrol. Rick and Kate were not just colleagues of Ben's dad, they were close family friends. Steve Harper was anxious to help in the search.

'I'd like to come with you, Rick, if I can just get my mountain gear together.' Rick Edwards had to make a decision.

'There isn't time, Steve, and in any case it's perhaps best if you leave this one to us. You're too closely involved.' Kate Jensen could see the desperation in Steve Harper's eyes but she knew it was the right decision.

'Rick's right, Steve. It's best if you stay down here. Sue is going to need your support. Don't worry, if Ben, Becky and the others are up there, we'll find them.'

In a prepared plan, each member of the team was allocated a sector of the mountain to be searched. From the main lift station they were carried up in a gondola to the ski area, high up above the resort. Each searcher was equipped with a powerful helmet light and a communication radio. The Snowcat machines were already up on the mountain, on the night shift, grooming the slopes for the next day's skiing. With their help, the rescue team was able to scour the slopes looking for any trace of the children. With the temperature dropping like a stone, this was a race against time.

Steve Harper waited in the control centre down below, listening to the crackle of the radios as each member of the search team updated the team leader on their progress. It was after midnight before the last member reported in. The whole mountain had been searched, as best they could in the conditions, and there was no sign of the children. It was time to call it a day. At first light, the search would begin again with fresh volunteers but, for now, there was nothing more they could do. In his head, Steve Harper kept going over all the possibilities. If Ben, Becky, Zoe and Sam were all missing, the chances are they were all together. If they were not in Silver Lake, or on the slopes above the resort, where else could they be? Little did he know, then, that they were indeed all together, but that the searchers were looking in the wrong place.

CHAPTER 10

High up on the glacier, a flicker of light came from the tiny window of the refuge. Sam leant forward and placed the last log on the fire. Becky was sound asleep, exhausted from the day's events. Ben had given her the spare fleece from his backpack and she was curled up with her head on Zoe's lap. Everyone else was dozing.

'That's the last log,' said Sam. Ben stirred.

'What's the time?' asked Ben. Carla checked her watch.

'It's after midnight. Do you think anyone's looking for us?'

'Of course they'll be looking,' said Ben, 'but will they know where to look?'

'They'll have sent out a search party by now,' said Sam, 'but they won't be looking up here on the glacier.

They may extend their search when it gets light. We'd better try to get some sleep. It could be a long day tomorrow.'

Ben made a pillow out of his backpack and tried, the best he could, to get comfortable. His brain was full of pictures, moving images of all the things that had happened to them during the day. Suddenly, he felt very tired and very sleepy. Zoe looked around the tiny room. The light from the wood stove flickered on the bare walls of the refuge whilst, outside, the wind and snow whistled around the building, as if trying to find a way in. Next to her, Marcus seemed to be asleep. Zoe stared at the fire, mesmerised by the flames licking around the last log. The lids of her eyes felt so heavy, she could hardly keep them open.

The next thing Zoe remembered was awakening with a start. The fire was almost out but there was still a gentle glow from the wooden embers. Then she realised what had woken her. There was the sound of quiet sobbing nearby but it wasn't coming from Becky. She was still sound asleep. Zoe got a torch out of her backpack and shone it around the room. Everyone seemed to be asleep.

The crying stopped. Marcus lifted his head and squinted in the light of the torch. He rubbed his eyes.

'Marcus,' said Zoe, 'are you awake?'

'Yes,' said Marcus, 'I couldn't sleep.' Zoe sat up and looked across at him in the dim light. She realised it was Marcus who had been crying.

'It's going to be alright, you know. If we all just stick together, things will work out.' Marcus was silent for a moment as if thinking what to say. When he spoke, he took Zoe by surprise.

'No, it's not going to work out,' he said. 'Everything is ruined.'

'What do mean?' said Zoe. 'We'll get through this and things will be back to normal, you'll see.'

'No, it will never be the same again.' The tone of Marcus' voice seemed both hopeless and angry. This was not the confident Marcus she knew. Zoe was curious.

'Why do you say that?'

'Because it's over,' said Marcus. 'We're leaving.' Zoe was now confused.

'Who's leaving?'

'My mum and I are leaving Forest Ridge. They're splitting up - my mum and dad are splitting up.'

'I'm sorry,' said Zoe. 'Why didn't you say?'

'No-one cares what I think,' said Marcus. 'No-one cares about me but you'll see, they'll be sorry.' With that Marcus turned away and laid his head back down on his backpack.

Zoe sat there in the dim light of her torch thinking of what Marcus had just said. Beside him lay the ski map he had used to lead them over the mountain from Eagle Summit. She picked it up and opened it out. With her torch, she followed the route they had taken from Sugar Bowl to Crystal Rock and then up to Eagle Summit. From there, Marcus had marked a red line across the base of the glacier and down Shepherds' Gully into Silver Lake. It all seemed such a long time ago and, yet, it was just yesterday. As she stared at the map, Zoe thought about how small they all were compared to the size of the mountain.

Then, suddenly, she noticed something that didn't make sense. There was another line drawn on the map using the same red pen, a line that stretched from Glacier Station across the top of the glacier and back down to Eagle Summit. Zoe stared at that red line and the truth began to dawn on her. Marcus had planned this in advance. He must have planned to take them to Silver Lake and then lead them from Glacier Station back across the glacier to Forest Ridge. Folding up the map, she laid it beside Marcus and switched off her torch. There in the darkness, she tried to make sense of what she had just discovered, but, for now, she was just too tired. Laying down her head, she drifted off to sleep, taking the secret she had discovered with her. There would be time to deal with it in the morning.

The next thing she remembered was daylight streaming through the tiny window and Becky asking for a drink. The fire had gone out and there was a chill in the air. Gradually, one by one, they began to stir and stretch their aching limbs. The hard stone floor was now just unforgiving and painful. Ben got up and stamped his feet to try to restore the circulation. Even though he had unclamped his boots, his feet still felt numb and as heavy as lead. Sam opened his eyes and sat up.

'Wakey, wakey, everyone,' he said jokingly, 'it's time to get up.'

'What time is it?' said Carla. 'I feel terrible.' Ben checked his watch.

'It's time we were up,' said Ben. 'We'll have to make the most of the daylight.' Ben went to the door of the refuge and, after a bit of a struggle, managed to heave it open. Outside, low cloud shrouded the whole mountain. The wind had dropped and it had stopped snowing. He took a deep breath of the cold morning air into his lungs. It made him cough. It was strangely quiet on the mountain, any sounds muffled by the low cloud and mist.

After they had all dipped into the remains of their packed lunches, the children sat down in a circle in the centre of the room.

'So, what's the plan?' said Ben.

'Well, we can't just sit here waiting to be rescued,' said Sam. 'Without a fire, we are all going to get very cold.' Zoe looked at Sam.

'How far is it from here to Eagle Summit, Sam?' Sam got out his map and laid it on the stone floor.

'Well, let's see. We're here at the refuge. That's about half way between Glacier Station and Eagle Summit.'

'How long do you reckon it would take us to reach Eagle Summit?' asked Zoe.

'Maybe, two hours,' said Sam, 'provided there are no snags.'

'I've had a look outside,' said Ben. 'The visibility is poor. Do you think we can make it without losing our way?' Sam fished the compass out of his backpack. He laid it down on the direction arrows and again carefully rotated the map to align it with north. With his small ruler and Marcus' red pen, he drew a straight line between the refuge and Eagle Summit.

'Now,' said Sam, 'if we just take a bearing from here to Eagle Summit, we shouldn't be far off.' Sam rotated the compass arrow to point towards Eagle Summit, keeping the red needle on magnetic north. 'There,' he said, 'that's the direction we need to follow.' He raised his hand from the map and pointed through the wall of the refuge.

'If you say so,' said Marcus who had been looking on quietly. 'When can we get going?'

'There's a problem,' said Ben. 'This is a glacier. We just don't know what lies under the snow. There are crevasses everywhere.'

'Is that not just a chance we're going to have to take?' said Zoe. Sam suddenly had an idea. He scrambled to his feet and went over to the wall cupboard where he'd found the lighter. He stretched up and lifted something off a nail on the back of the door.

'How about this?' he cried. 'I spotted it last night.' In his hand Sam held a coil of climbing rope. 'Look,' he said, 'some climbers must have left it behind. See, some of the outer braiding has been torn so they probably didn't want to risk using it but it will do us just fine.'

'What do you mean?' said Carla.

'Simple,' said Sam. 'We rope ourselves together. That way we won't get lost and if the worst happens - well, let's not think about that.'

'Right,' said Ben, 'I vote we take Sam's advice. We've got to try to help ourselves.' They all looked at each other and, one by one, they nodded in agreement, even Becky and she didn't understand any of it.

Slowly, they gathered up all their belongings and packed them away in their backpacks. Sam found a piece of cord and tied the compass securely to one of the shoulder straps. That way he could use it to check on their direction without fear of dropping it. There was also one last thing he wanted to do before leaving the refuge. Sam took the precious lighter and returned it to the plastic bag in the cupboard. Ben then scribbled a message on the note they had found and left it with the lighter. Someone else might be glad of it.

Outside, they bolted the door of the refuge, clamped on their skis and lined up one behind the other, making sure Becky was between Zoe and Ben.

'Do you mind if I lead?' said Marcus. Sam looked at him for a moment.

'Yes, why not?' said Sam. 'Just so long as I can come behind you to check on our direction. Before Ben attached his skis, he uncoiled the climbing rope and wrapped it first around Marcus' waist, securing it with a knot. Leaving a bit of slack, he then attached it to Sam before passing the rope around Zoe and Becky. When he had tied himself on, he passed the remainder of the rope to Carla to secure herself.

'Okay, everyone,' shouted Sam, 'let's take it nice and slowly. There's no rush. Right, Marcus, that way.' With his arm outstretched, Sam pointed straight ahead. As he kept a careful eye on the compass, the group disappeared off into the mist, leaving the refuge behind. Little did they know, it would be another eventful day.

CHAPTER 11

'Can you tell me his full name, please?'

'It's Marcus - Marcus King.'

'And your daughter's name?'

'It's Carla, with a C - Carla Martin.' The police officer looked up from his desk.

'Thank you. Tell me, have they ever gone missing or run away before?' Jill Martin looked a bit uneasy.

'Well, she has missed school a few times but never anything like this. She's never stayed away overnight before.' The police officer seemed thoughtful.

'You see, Mrs Martin, I've been on to the senior school in Bridgeton. Apparently, both Marcus and your daughter were at registration yesterday morning but no-one has seen them since.' Phil King sat upright, clearly angry.

'What, you mean they've been missing since yesterday morning? Why did no-one tell us?' The police officer tried to calm the situation.

'I suppose no-one noticed they had left the school. It does happen, especially near the end of term. Tell me, is there any reason why Marcus might run away from home? Has there been any problem or argument?' Phil and Angela King shifted uncomfortably in their chairs.

'Well, you know what boys are like, Officer. They have their ups and downs.' Phil King was not entirely convincing. Police Officer Joe Barnes looked at Angela King and raised his eyebrows.

'Mrs King?'

'Well, actually, there has been a bit of an upset in the family recently, Officer. My husband and I are planning on splitting up - at least for a while. I'm leaving Forest Ridge and moving down to Bridgeton with Marcus.' The officer waited patiently.

'And how does your son feel about that?' Phil and Angela King exchanged a glance before Phil King answered.

'Marcus was very unhappy about it. He doesn't want to leave Forest Ridge.'

'Right,' said the police officer after a moment, 'what I'd like you all to do is go home and check that Marcus and Carla haven't returned. They may have stayed with friends last night but we usually find they return home when they're hungry or their money runs out. Oh, and if you wouldn't mind checking to see if they have taken anything unusual from the house. That may give us a clue and, in the meantime, we'll alert all our patrol cars to keep a look out for them in Bridgeton. Here's my number if you find out anything you think may help in the search.'

With that the meeting ended; the worried parents left the Forest Ridge Police Station and went their separate ways. When he had finished the paperwork, Police Officer Joe Barnes took the incident form through to his assistant for logging on the police computer.

'You know,' he said, 'that's two groups of missing children in just twenty four hours. First there were those four young skiers and now this pair of teenagers. I reckon it's going to be a busy day.' The assistant looked up from her keyboard.

'Have they made any progress tracking down the youngsters?'

'Well, they were out on the mountain till late last night and drew a blank. They are continuing the search this morning but with the low cloud and heavy snow, it's not going to be easy.' The assistant shook her head in sympathy.

'Their poor parents,' she said. 'They must be out of their minds with worry.'

At that moment the desk phone rang. Joe Barnes picked it up.

'Joe Barnes, Forest Ridge Police Station. Mr King, any news? His skis? Thank you that's very helpful.' Joe Barnes hung up and dialled the number on the form in front of him. 'Mrs Martin? It's Police Officer Barnes, Forest Ridge here. Tell me, are Carla's skis still in the house? If you could, I'll hang on.' Joe Barnes looked at his assistant as he waited. His eyes said everything. 'Hello, Mrs Martin - I see, you've checked and they're not there. Thank you, that's very helpful. No, don't worry, I'll get back in touch if I have any news.' With that he hung up. 'This looks like a bigger problem than I first thought. Get on to the mountain rescue team and let them know the situation. It looks like they may now be looking for six missing children on the mountain.'

Up at the rescue control centre things were starting to move fast. A special task force had been set up to gather all available CCTV recordings from Forest Ridge and Silver Lake. There were many hours of digital footage to check through so it wasn't going to be an easy task. How could four children - or now possibly six youngsters - disappear without trace? Marked up on a white board were their names - Ben and Becky Harper, Zoe Roberts and Sam Fletcher. The names of Marcus King and Carla Martin had been added to list, with question marks beside them. In a small room next to the control centre sat Steve and Sue Harper, Pam Roberts and Jack Fletcher, anxiously waiting for any news. The breakthrough came just after midday.

'I think we've got footage of them,' called an excited member of the team. 'It's from a camera at the cable car station at Crystal Rock.' The four parents rushed into the control room to see the CCTV recording.

'Yes, that's them,' said Steve Harper, 'Ben, Zoe and Sam but what were they doing up at Crystal Rock? They were supposed to be going to Silver Lake after they had taken Becky to the holiday club at Sugar Bowl.' The search team leader was studying the screen.

'Who are these two?' he asked pointing to a taller boy and girl beside them. Ben's dad recognised Marcus immediately.

'That's Marcus King. His father owns the ski store at the centre of the village. I'm not sure about the girl.' Rick Edwards, the team leader, swung into action.

'Alright, someone get in touch with the parents of the other two children and get them up here as soon as possible. If they travelled up to Eagle Summit from Crystal Rock, we should be able to track them back down again with the cameras on the mountain and see where they went after that. As quick as you can, let's get on to it.'

With some hard evidence to go on, everyone's spirits were lifted. Now at least they had a starting point. Throughout the afternoon, every piece of CCTV footage was checked for the next clue as to the whereabouts of the children but in the end they drew a blank. Once again, their spirits began to fall. There was just no sign of them in Forest Ridge. Rick Edwards paced up and down the control room, racking his brain for the answer. Suddenly, a thought came to him. Maybe they were looking in the wrong place.

'Let's start looking at the CCTV footage from Silver Lake. They may have gone there after all.' One of team spoke up.

'But we've already checked the recordings from the bus station. They never got on the bus to Silver Lake.'

'Never mind,' he said. 'I've had a thought. Let's just check the footage from Silver Lake.' The children's parents waited, hoping for that tiny piece of information that would help solve the mystery. When it came, it was as unexpected as it was puzzling and they all crowded once more into the control room, peering at the playback monitor. The identification markings at the bottom of the

CCTV footage showed it was taken from a camera in the entrance hall of the funicular railway station in Silver Lake - the rail tunnel link to Glacier Station, the highest point in the area.

'I don't believe it,' said Ben's dad. 'It's them, all of them, Ben, Becky and all the others but how on earth did they manage to get to Silver Lake?' Rick Edwards, the team leader, was matter of fact in his response.

'I think they've skied to Silver Lake from the top of Eagle Summit.'

'What?' said Zoe's mum. 'You mean they've gone out of bounds?'

'That's what I reckon.' He picked up a wooden pointer and traced it across the large scale map on the wall. 'I think they've skied from Eagle Summit, across the base of the glacier and down Shepherds' Gully into Silver Lake.' Sam's dad was still trying to make sense of it.

'But if they got to Silver Lake and travelled on the funicular up to Glacier Station, why have we not found them on the slopes above Silver Lake?' Rick Edwards was silent for a moment, staring at the map. In his head he knew that there was one possible explanation why the children had not yet been found but it was so worrying, for now, he decided to keep it to himself. However, when he spoke, his instructions were clear to everyone.

'Continue checking for any CCTV footage of the children in Silver Lake to make sure we haven't missed anything.' He paused for a moment before continuing. 'And let's get a search team up on the train to Glacier Station as soon as possible.'

CHAPTER 12

Roped together for safety, the small group of children continued across the glacier. At times they would catch a glimpse of Eagle Summit ahead of them. Then, suddenly, a bank of cloud would sweep in, engulfing them in a grey blanket. Trying to ski blind was almost impossible and, at times, Marcus had to slow to a snail's pace. Behind him, Sam kept an eye on his compass, occasionally shouting instructions to aim a bit to the right or left. The others just hung on to the rope putting their trust in those up front. After more than an hour, Marcus brought them to a halt and they all slumped down in the snow. With the visibility so poor, their progress was slow. Marcus turned to the others to speak, his voice strangely muffled by the mist.

'The rope is slowing us up. I think we should untie ourselves and ski on our own.'

'No,' said Zoe, 'we must stay together. If we untie the rope, someone could get lost in this cloud.' Ben agreed.

'Zoe is right. Even if we are making slow progress, we must stay together for everyone's safety.'

'How much further do you think we have to go?' said Carla. Sam shook his head.

'It's hard to say but if we just keep heading in the right direction, we should reach Eagle Summit before dark. That's all we can hope for.'

'Right,' said Ben, 'then that's what we have to do. Let's keep moving. If we stay here, we'll freeze.'

Slowly, they struggled back to their feet, stamping their skis to warm their aching muscles. Marcus set off once more. He tried to build up some speed, pulling on the rope to encourage them to ski faster, impatient to make better progress. The others followed in a line, sometimes closing up on one another, sometimes stretching apart like a long wriggling caterpillar. It was cold, tiring and monotonous, so when the crisis came, no-one was expecting it.

One second the rope connecting them was slack, the next it snapped tight with a force that knocked the breath out of them.

'Hold on!' screamed Ben. Ahead of him, Sam was being dragged across the ice pulled by a heavy weight. Zoe spread her skis in a wide snowplough but it was no use. The pull was too great. Her bindings broke loose and she was catapulted forward. Ben edged his skis sharply and, throwing all his weight backwards, he dug them into the snow.

'What's happened?' screamed Becky. 'What's happened?' Suddenly, the rope went very taught and they shuddered to a halt. At least they had stopped sliding.

'Hang on, everyone!' shouted Ben. 'Dig in your skis or boots and don't let it slide any further. Marcus, what's happening? Are you okay?' There was no reply. Zoe could see Sam straining on the rope. In front of them a gap had opened up in the ice and Marcus had disappeared. With the jarring tug, Sam's skis had broken free and now his boots were braced against the jaws of the crevasse, as he struggled to stop himself from being pulled in. Below him, Marcus swung on the end of the rope. He could see there was nothing but icy darkness beneath him.

'I can't hold him much longer,' said Sam. 'He's too heavy.' Ben knew they couldn't just give up.

'Marcus, try to get a foothold. Try to dig your boots into the ice. You've got to take some of the strain.'

'It's no use,' said Sam. 'He can't seem to get a grip.' Ben kept trying.

'Tell him to get the soles of his boots up against the wall of the crevasse and wedge his back against the other side.' Inside the gap in the rock, Marcus could hear Ben's instructions but, with the shock of falling through the snow, it was difficult to think straight. When he realised what had happened, he started to panic, fighting to gain a foothold on the icy walls so that he could brace himself against the sides of the chasm. At last, he managed to get enough of a foothold to take the strain off the rope.

'Quick, Sam,' said Ben. 'Make a loop in rope, stick both your ski poles through it and lay them across the gap to take the strain. Instinctively, Sam knew what to do. He pulled the rope tight around his ski poles and laid them across the mouth of the crevasse. They were just long enough to reach and now, at least, Marcus wouldn't fall any further. With that done, there was enough slack on the rope for the others to untie themselves, pulling the rope up and over their heads. Ben crawled forwards on all fours and looked over the edge. Marcus was wedged in a bottleneck of ice. Beneath him, the yawning gap disappeared down into the depths of the mountain.

'Marcus,' said Ben, 'we're going to get you out but you've got to help.' Marcus looked up in desperation.

'I can't,' he said. 'I haven't got any strength left.' Zoe scrambled over and peered down. She needed to act fast.

'Listen, Marcus,' said Zoe. 'Stop feeling sorry for yourself. You can do this. You've got to try.' Zoe turned to Carla. 'Carla, I need your help. Bring the end of the rope over here.' Carla did as she was told and crawled over to Zoe's side. 'Right, Carla, I want you to lower the end loop of the rope down to Marcus. Get it as close to his boot as possible.' Carla followed her instructions. Zoe looked down at Marcus' upturned face. She had never seen him look so scared but she tried to stay calm. 'Now,

Marcus, I want you to get the toe of your boot through the loop in the rope.'

As Marcus moved his footing, he slipped slightly. They all gasped but the ski poles held secure. Eventually, after several tries, he succeeded in hooking his toe into the dangling rope loop.

'Now, Marcus,' said Zoe, 'when we take the strain, I want you to stand up.' All the others scrambled to get a grip of the rope. 'Now,' said Zoe, 'grab the rope and stand up.' Marcus hauled himself up. It was only a small distance but it was something. 'Right, now brace yourself against the wall again to take the strain off the rope.' Marcus followed Zoe's instructions. When the children had pulled in some more slack, he stood up again and raised himself a little bit higher. Slowly, but surely, he was making progress. After what seemed like an age, Marcus' head was eventually level with the edge of the crevasse. He was exhausted with the effort but Zoe was not going to let him give up.

'Right, Marcus,' said Zoe, 'you're almost there. Just one more step.' Summoning up the last of his strength, the children pulled in the rope and Marcus hauled himself up one last time. Ben and Sam quickly reached down and grabbed him under his arms. With one mighty effort, they all managed to drag him over the lip of the crevasse and back onto solid ground. For a moment, no-one had the energy to speak. They all just lay there panting in the snow, drained but triumphant. It was Becky who broke the silence.

'Look,' she said, 'there it is.' For a brief moment the mist had cleared, and there, ahead of them, was the familiar outline of Eagle Summit. The huge structure of the top cable car station stood out against the sky, sitting securely on the summit. They could make out the cable car hanging from its cradle in the loading bay, and beside it was the steeply pitched roof of the Eagle's Nest Café. Ben jumped to his feet to get a better view and Sam checked his compass. His direction finding had not been far off.

'Quick,' said Ben, 'let's press on. We're almost there.' It was then that Marcus gave them the bad news.

'I've lost my skis,' he said. 'The bindings broke when I fell. They're down at the bottom of the crevasse. You'll have to go on ahead without me. I'll follow on foot. I don't want to hold you up.' Ben was having none of it.

'Listen, Marcus, we're in this together so we stick together.' Ben handed him one of his skis.

'Here, stick your best foot in this. I'll do the adjustments.' Marcus took the ski whilst Ben knelt down and moved the rear binding to fit Marcus' boot. He then snapped it shut with the palm of his hand. 'There, that should do it,' said Ben. Marcus seemed embarrassed and unsure.

'But, Ben, that leaves you with only one ski.'

'Good,' said Ben, 'we can have a competition to see who's best at skiing with only one ski. Now, let's rope up again and, Marcus, try to give us some warning if you plan to fall into any more crevasses.'

The cloud swept in once more, shrouding Eagle Summit in mist but, by now, they were pretty sure of their bearings. The top station was straight ahead if only they could keep going. Sliding forward, one behind the other, the bedraggled group continued on their way, with Marcus and Ben both balancing on a downhill ski, their other boot swinging like a pendulum through the snow. Before long the great shadow of the Eagle Summit top station loomed out of the mist in front of them. They had made it but they still had a short climb ahead of them if they were to reach their goal.

One by one, they undid their skis and untied the rope. It had served them well. When they were all ready, they shouldered their skis and started to climb. It was strenuous work. The altitude left them with little spare oxygen and the muscles in their legs ached. They had to stop every few minutes for a breather but, at last, they were there, standing outside the top station. It was closed down, deserted, shut up tight against the weather. The children climbed the metal steps to the loading platform, bracing themselves against the wind. The top cable car swung gently in the loading bay, its doors firmly sealed against the elements. Marcus tried the main door into the building. It was locked and shuttered, abandoned by skiers and staff in the face of the storm. There seemed to be no way in.

'What do we do now?' asked Carla. 'How do we get inside?'

'We could try breaking a window,' said Marcus.

'These outside windows are made of plate glass,' said Ben. 'We'd need a sledge hammer to have any chance.' Sam wasn't for giving up.

'There's always a way to get in,' he said. 'You just have to look for it.' Sam laid down his skis and disappeared around the side of the building. Everyone else just sat down on the steps, huddled together for warmth. The wind whistled around the tangled metal structure as they all grew colder and colder. Zoe noticed a tiny spot of frostnip on the tip of Becky's nose, the first sign of danger. She covered it with her glove to bring back the circulation. By the time Sam returned they were all beginning to lose any feeling in their fingers and toes.

'I think we're in luck,' he said. 'Get your gear and follow me.' The children followed Sam around the side of the building, stumbling down some steps towards a side door. It was bolted, with a padlock hanging nearby but, luckily, in their rush to close down the top station, someone had forgotten to secure the padlock. Sam pulled back the bolt and pushed open the heavy, metal door. It was dark inside and there was a strong smell of oil. Zoe switched on her torch and swung it around the basement room. There were pipes and bundles of cables attached to the walls, some heavy machinery with switches and dials and a row of metal oil drums. In the corner, she spotted a short flight of stairs leading up to another door.

'This way,' she said, 'follow me.' In the light of Zoe's torch, the children made their way across the concrete floor and up the staircase. Zoe put her hand on the door handle and looked around at the others. 'Here's hoping we're in luck,' she said. She pushed down on the handle and tried the door. It was unlocked and opened into a long corridor. Daylight flooded down on them from a skylight up above. They were into the main building. So far, so good. They were inside and out of the cold.

Moving through the deserted complex, gave them a strange feeling. They were glad to have reached shelter but they also felt a bit like intruders. Another set of steps led them past the cable car control room. It was locked. Through the glass window they could see the switches and computer system that controlled the lift.

'Maybe if we could get inside, we could get the cable car working,' said Carla. Marcus tried a light switch but nothing happened.

'It's no use,' he said. 'The power is off. The whole place is shut down. Carla, have you tried your phone again?' Carla got the phone out of her pocket and powered it up. Everyone waited in hope. For a moment it flickered into life. The battery low symbol flashed for a few seconds and, then, the power shut down.

'Oh no,' said Carla, 'the battery's dead. What are we going to do now?'

'It's the cold,' said Ben. 'It kills the batteries. We'll just have to think of some other way to get help.'

'Do you think they're still looking for us?' said Becky. Ben knew a search team would be out looking for them but how would they know where to start?

'Of course they'll be looking for us,' said Ben. 'Dad will make sure of that. Don't you worry, they'll find us.' But Ben was worried because he knew they had to get through at least another night. There was little heat in the

building and they had no food left. What were they going
to do?

CHAPTER 13

In the entrance hall of the funicular station, the rescue team was making final preparations. Kate Jensen was in charge. She knew the glacier like the back of her hand but she also knew the search wasn't going to be easy.

'Okay, listen up, everyone. When we get up to Glacier Station, we won't have much daylight left so we need to make best use of our time. Any questions?' A voice spoke up at the back of the group. It was Ben's dad, Steve Harper.

'I'd like to come with you, Kate. If Ben and the others are out there, I want to be able to help.'

'I don't know if that's a good idea, Steve. You're too closely involved.' Steve Harper pushed through to the front of the group to press his case.

'I can help. If you find any of their equipment, I may be able to identify it. You said it yourself, time is all important.' Kate Jensen considered what he had just said and realised that his inside knowledge might prove to be useful. She decided to accept his offer.

'Okay, you can come but, please, no heroics. This search is going to be dangerous enough.'

Kate Jensen turned to the control room window and gave the thumbs up. Glacier Station had been closed since the storm blew in. This would be the first journey back up. The emergency doors sealing the tunnel entrance slid open and the rescue team climbed aboard the train. For once, it was strangely empty. When all was ready, the warning bell sounded and the automatic doors of the carriages slid shut. The driver powered up and the train pulled slowly away from the base station, clamped to the accelerating drag cable. In no time, it was up to speed and climbing rapidly through the tunnel of rock.

The journey up to Glacier Station would take less than ten minutes but, in their eagerness to get to the top, it seemed to take longer than usual. When the search team exited the top station, visibility was variable. One minute it was clear, then the next a bank of cloud would sweep in and engulf the mountain. Kate Jensen waited patiently for the mist to clear. When it did, she had her binoculars ready. Focusing down on the glacier, she used them to scan for any signs of life. The rest of the team did the same, searching for any movement, or unusual colour, on the sea of ice below them. It was Ben's dad who was the first to spot something.

'Look, over there,' he shouted. He was pointing at something orange caught on jagged rocks below them in the distance. Kate Jensen followed the direction of his outstretched arm and zoomed in on the area with her binoculars. She saw it flapping in the wind, but at that distance it could be anything.

'Let's take a closer look,' she said. 'It may be nothing but we'd better make sure.' The team clamped on their skis and fell in behind the team leader. She was an experienced mountain guide and had a detailed knowledge of the glacier and its crevasses. If anyone could lead the group safely across its icy slopes, it was her. Dropping down the back of Glacier Station, Kate Jensen led the search team in the direction of the flapping orange material, whatever it might be. The snow was deep so they had to use short rhythmic turns to plough through the drifts to a point high above their target. Here the team leader halted to assess the danger.

The slope was steep and there had been a heavy build up of snow on the underlying base. It was likely to be unstable and the last thing they needed now was to set off an avalanche.

'Right,' she said, 'could everyone check that their transceiver is set to transmit.' Each member of the rescue team wore an electronic search device to help locate a buried casualty in the event of an avalanche. Kate Jensen continued with her instructions. 'Let's cross the next slope one at a time. There's no point in taking unnecessary risks.' Everyone knew the drill. If the slope was to give way, you would need some people to search and there was more chance of finding one person than a whole group. One by one the search team crossed the slope, only starting when they knew the skier ahead had reached safety. At last, they were all across.

As they approached the orange target, Ben's dad had a feeling of foreboding. When they reached it, one of the group undid his skis and clambered through the snow and rocks to where the orange material was caught, shredded by the wind. He undid it and brought it back to the group for inspection. Even in its torn state, there was no mistaking it. It was a lightweight tent that someone must have used on the glacier for shelter but whose tent was it and where were they now? Steve Harper recognised it immediately. When he spoke, it was with a sense of gloom.

'It's Ben's,' he said. 'It's Ben's tent. I bought it for him last year.' One of the team packed it away in a backpack. No-one knew what to say. It was left to the team leader to raise their spirits.

'Which means,' she said, 'they probably took shelter in it before moving on. Where do you think they would head to?'

'There's only one place I can think of,' said Ben's dad. 'The refuge, they may have tried to get to it.' Kate Jensen tried to sound positive.

'Well, let's check it out. They may be sheltering there.' Adjusting her backpack, she prepared to set off. 'The next section is dangerous,' she said. 'There are crevasses everywhere. Try to stay in my tracks.' Using her instinctive knowledge of the mountain to guide her, she began a long looping descent down the face of the glacier. Each member of the team followed behind, hardly deviating from her chosen line, well aware of the dangers that lay in wait for them beneath the snow. If they strayed even a few metres to the right or left, it could spell disaster.

Eventually, the outline of a small shelter appeared ahead of them. It was the refuge. The stone walls and corrugated, metal roof looked fragile but it had stood the test of time on the glacier, despite many severe winters. Ben's dad was out of his skis in an instant, wanting to end the suspense and find out if the children were inside but the team leader stopped him.

'Wait, Steve,' she said, 'let Dan check it out.' The other team member took off his skis and made his way around the building to the door. After a few minutes, he returned with something in his hand. He was shaking his head.

'There's nobody there,' he said. Everyone lowered their heads in disappointment. 'But there's been a fire lit in the stove recently and, look, I've found this.' He handed Kate Jensen a small plastic bag, containing a disposable lighter and a note. She read it out to the group.

'I leave this lighter to whoever finds it. It saved my life and I hope it saves yours.'

'It was probably left by a climber,' said Steve Harper. 'Was there any sign of the children?' Kate Jensen held up the note.

'There's more,' she said. 'Something has been added in a different hand.' Everyone crowded around to see. Yes, the handwriting was different, almost childlike, and it said: 'Thanks for the lighter, Ben'. Steve Harper grabbed the note to read it for himself. Yes, there was no mistaking it. It was Ben's handwriting. They must have made it to the refuge after all but where were they now?

Kate Jensen knew she had to make a decision. 'The light's going,' she said. We need to get off the glacier before dark. If they left the refuge, they may have headed off down towards Shepherds' Gully and Silver Lake.

That would be the most direct route off the glacier. Let's check it out and keep your eyes open for any clues.' With that they set off once more, snaking their way down the mountain in a controlled descent but it soon became obvious there was no sign of the missing children. By the time they reached Silver Lake it was almost dark. There was not much more they could do until tomorrow.

Outside the control centre a small crowd had gathered, eager for any news. Sue Harper was waiting for her husband. She hardly dared to ask.

'Any news?' she said. Steve Harper told her what he knew.

'It seems they spent last night at the refuge on the glacier.' He showed her the note with Ben's handwriting on it. 'There's still hope. We just have to keep searching.' Carla's mum had got the news but was still unable to take it all in.

'I don't understand it,' she said. 'I bought Carla a new phone for her birthday. I keep trying her number but it seems to be switched off.' Ben's dad tried to reassure her.

'Don't worry,' he said. 'Reception is not good on the glacier and, in any case, phone batteries will not last long in the cold. Trust me, no news is good news.'

CHAPTER 14

'I'm hungry,' said Becky. Ben had a look inside his sister's backpack.

'Don't you have any chocolate left that you could have?'

'We finished it this morning. Don't you remember?' Sam, Zoe, Ben, Marcus, Carla and Becky were sitting on the floor outside the cable car control room with their backs against the rough, concrete wall. It was cold but better than being outside. Marcus had an idea.

'What about the Eagle's Nest Café? There's bound to be something to eat in there.' The Eagle's Nest Café was built against the side of the Eagle Summit lift station. It was only open in good weather when the cable car was operating.

'I've checked,' said Sam. 'All the outside doors are securely fastened and the connecting door to the lift station is locked from inside the café. I've tried it.' Marcus was still thinking. He'd been in the café many times and he had just remembered something.

'What about the ventilation windows?'

'The what?' said Carla. Marcus appeared excited.

'The ventilation windows - I've just remembered, there are four small windows high up on the connecting wall between the café and the lift station. They're usually open during the summer months to keep the café cool.' Zoe seemed interested.

'So how do we get to them?' Marcus looked around him to try to get his bearings.

'They must be up on the next level.' He got to his feet. 'Come on, let's see if we can find them.'

Marcus led the way as they all climbed the stairs to the top floor and a short corridor that was dimly lit in the failing light. He wasn't mistaken. There, on the corridor wall, just above head height, were four tiny windows.

'Here, Sam,' said Marcus. 'Have a look and see if we are above the café.' Marcus tapped his knee to show Sam where to place his foot. Sam eased himself up and swung onto Marcus' shoulders so that he could see down through one of the windows.

'Yes,' said Sam, 'it's the café alright. I can see the tables and chairs.'

'See if the window will open,' said Marcus. Sam pressed against the frame of the first window. It was firmly closed. But Sam was not for giving up.

'Move along and I'll try the next one.' Marcus took a few steps to the right, carefully balancing Sam on his shoulders. Sam tried again, banging the heel of his gloved hand against the window frame. It creaked and moved a little.

'Try it again,' said Marcus. As Sam hit the window frame again, a small gap opened up and he was able to get his hand inside and push the window open to about forty five degrees. He put his head into the narrow gap and peered down into the café below. It looked a long way down. He slid down from Marcus' shoulders.

'What do you think, Sam?' said Zoe. 'Is it possible to get into the café?' Sam shook his head.

'The gap in the window is just too narrow and it's a long way down.'

'What about using the rope?' suggested Zoe. 'We still have it.' Although he still had his doubts, Sam was prepared to have a go. Carla offered to go and collect the rope from down in the basement where they had left it. When she returned, Sam had taken off his ski boots and thick ski jacket. It was going to be a tight fit so he wanted to give himself every chance. Tying the rope around his waist, he climbed back up on Marcus' shoulders. Then, holding onto the window frame above him, he carefully stood up and slipped one leg through the narrow gap. Marcus held his free hand to steady him as he tried to squeeze his other leg through the window. It was just too narrow. In the end, Marcus and the others had to ease Sam back down to the floor.

'It's no use,' gasped Sam. 'The gap is just too narrow.' After so much hope, everyone was silent, their spirits deflated. It was Becky who spoke up.

'I bet I could do it.' Ben was quick to answer her.

'Don't be silly, Becky, you're too young and it's too dangerous.'

'But I'm the only one small enough to fit through the gap,' said Becky, 'and, anyway, I'm not scared to do it.' The children all looked at each other.

'She's got a point,' said Marcus. Ben still wasn't sure.

'It's too dangerous. What if she falls? And, anyway, she may not be able to unlock the door even if she gets down safely.'

'I know I can do it,' said Becky. 'Please, let me try.' Marcus seemed to agree.

'It's okay, Ben, she'll be tightly tied on to the rope. If it doesn't work we can simply forget it.'

So that's how the decision to use Becky was made. It was obvious, however, that they would need a more stable platform to work from. Sam remembered he had seen a table down in the basement switch room. He went off with Zoe and Carla to bring it up from below. Ben helped Becky to take off her ski boots and jacket and Marcus carefully tied the rope around her waist. When the others returned carrying the table, they pushed it up against the wall beneath the window. When Ben had checked that the knot was secure, Zoe, Sam and Carla took a firm grip of the rope. Marcus and Ben climbed up on the table so that their shoulders were level with the window and lifted Becky up beside them.

'Okay, Becky, are you still sure you want to do this?' said Ben. 'You don't have to.'

'Of course I do,' said Becky. 'Let's get on with it.' Ben and Marcus hoisted her up and Becky slipped her stockinged feet through the gap in the window.

'Right, Becky,' said Ben, 'now turn over onto your tummy so that we can lower you down with your face to the wall.' Becky rolled over and slipped slowly through the gap. It was a tight fit but eventually she was through, turning her head sideways to clear the window frame.

'Now, let the rope out slowly,' said Marcus, 'very slowly.' Gradually, Becky began to slide down the inside wall of the café. It was a long way down. Marcus peered through the gap in the window frame, trying to judge, in the failing light, how far she still had to go. 'I think she's almost there,' said Marcus. 'Give her a bit more slack.' As they loosened their grip on the rope, Becky fell the last short distance and landed with a thud on the tiled floor.

'Ouch,' she shouted, 'that hurt.'

'Are you alright, Becky?' called Ben.

'Yes, I think so. I just twisted my ankle when I landed. What do I do now?'

'Try to find the connecting door to the lift station. It should be nearby.' Becky got up and half limped, half crawled towards the two doors she had spotted. The faraway door had a sign above it saying toilets downstairs. The nearest one was marked private and it was locked. She could already hear someone knocking from the other side.

'Hold on,' she said, 'I'm trying, I'm trying.' Turning the locking catch to the right, she moved back and waited. The door burst open and there was Sam with the others crowded behind him.

'Well done, Becky, you're a hero!' said Sam. 'Sorry, heroine.' Everyone piled through into the café, excited by the thought of finding something to eat. It was only Carla who noticed that Becky was crouching awkwardly on one leg.

'Here,' she said, 'let me help you. You probably just twisted it when you landed.' Carla scooped Becky up and carried her over to a padded bench seat in the corner beside the empty open fire. 'Wait here and I'll see what I can find for your ankle.'

With the café and lift station closed up, there weren't any fresh food stuffs to be found in the kitchen. However, there was still a stock of dried and tinned food available. Sam had found what he was looking for, some matches, old newspapers and a supply of logs. He wasted no time in getting a fire going. Zoe and Ben found a box of candles in a drawer and some candle-holders arranged on a shelf. In no time, the inside of the Eagle's Nest Café was bathed in warm, flickering light. When Carla returned she had a plastic bag full of snow. She wrapped it in a cloth and placed it on Becky's injured ankle.

'There,' she said, 'that should help to keep the swelling down.'

Inside the kitchen, Marcus was trying to make sense of the equipment. Some of it required electrical power but that was switched off. However, there were also some gas burners. He tried lighting one of them with some matches but he had no luck.

'The gas supply must also be switched off,' said Zoe. 'I'll check it out.' It didn't take her long to find what she was looking for. In a back room there was a supply of bottled gas connected to a network of pipes. Zoe turned the red handle on the top of the first tank in the direction of the arrow and called through to Marcus in the kitchen.

'Try it now, Marcus. It may take a minute.' Marcus turned on one of the gas controls, struck a match and carefully held the flame over the burner. After a few seconds, he heard a hiss of gas and it lit with a loud popping sound. They were now in business.

'Let's see what we can find to eat,' said Zoe. 'There's a storeroom through the back.' Taking a candle in its holder, Zoe and Marcus went to see what they could find. Arranged neatly on the shelves were sealed packets of dried pasta and assorted tins. She handed Marcus three packets of pasta and two large tins of tuna, before gathering up some tinned tomatoes and a large can of mixed bean salad.

'This will do for starters,' she said. 'It's not what I would normally choose, but at least we won't go hungry.' Back in the kitchen they were joined by Ben and Carla.

'Sam's getting a fire going,' said Ben. 'Is there anything I can do to help?'

'Yes,' said Zoe, 'we need to get a large pot of water boiling on the stove for this pasta and Carla can you find some pots to heat the tomatoes and bean salad?' Everyone had a job to do except Becky. Ben had an idea. Once he had the water on the heat, he went through to the café to find Sam. They pushed two of the tables together close to the fire and set out six chairs. Then, between them, Ben and Sam carried Becky through to the kitchen and lifted her onto a high stool. The water was coming to the boil.

'Now, Becky,' said Ben, 'we need you to time the pasta so that it's properly cooked.' He selected the stopwatch function on his wristwatch and handed it to Becky. After he had sprinkled some salt into the boiling water, he tore open the packets of dried pasta and emptied the contents into the pot.

'Right, Becky,' he said, 'start the stopwatch now and tell me when twelve minutes have passed.' Becky already knew what to do. She had often helped her mum with cooking times at home.

Sam found some soap and washed the dirt from his hands before helping Zoe carry some plates and cutlery through to the table in the café. They even discovered some napkins, and Zoe decorated the table with four more candles. Marcus had also found assorted cans of soft drinks in the storeroom which he placed around the table, along with six glasses from a side cupboard.

'Ten minutes,' said Becky. 'Just two minutes to go.' Ben gave the pot a stir and lifted a large colander from a hook in the kitchen. He tasted a bit of the pasta to check if it was properly cooked. 'Time's up,' said Becky. 'I'm starving.' Ben drained off the pasta and tipped it into a huge serving bowl, before carrying it through to the table in the café. Carla and Zoe brought through the tuna, tomatoes and mixed beans, while Marcus and Sam switched off all the gas burners and carried Becky through to her chair at the table.

Never before could a group have sat down to such an improvised meal under such unusual circumstances. The serving dishes were passed around and they filled their plates in almost near silence. It was the strangest, most bizarre meal any of them could remember but, at that moment, the food never tasted so good. Out of the blue, Becky posed a question that took them all by surprise.

'Will the owners of the café mind us eating their food?' she said. 'I mean, we haven't paid for any of it.' All the others just looked at her. None of them had even given this a thought. They were all just too hungry to care. Zoe tried to explain.

'I think they'll understand that this is an emergency, Becky, but of course we will offer to pay for it all when we get the chance.' This seemed to satisfy her.

Outside the Eagle's Nest Café the wind continued to howl and the snow fell heavily, but inside they were warm and safe, at least for the present. At the end of the meal, to everyone's surprise, Carla produced a large bowl of tinned peaches in syrup, a perfect end to a not so perfect day. When they had all eaten their fill, Ben raised his glass of cola.

'To our safe return,' said Ben, 'and to everyone for sticking together.' At that moment, they all felt sure that they had come through the worst and, in the morning, they were confident they would be found and rescued. Just one more night and this adventure would be behind them. After all, what else could go wrong?

CHAPTER 15

A small crowd of onlookers had gathered outside Forest Ridge Junior School. Earlier in the day a television crew had arrived along with a mobile satellite broadcast unit. The local police were on hand to keep order, and Joe Barnes had been appointed their spokesperson. The crowd was pushing forward for a better view so he tried to move them back.

'Okay, everyone, if we could all just stand back a bit and let the television crew get on with their business.' Police officer or not, Joe Barnes was not looking forward to the broadcast. They had six children missing on the mountain and the local media had picked up on the story. Now he was going to be interviewed live on the Evening News and there wasn't a lot he was going to be able to tell them. All they knew was that the youngsters were still somewhere up on the glacier.

A telecommunications engineer had already raised the satellite dish on the roof of the mobile unit. Inside the van he was making the final adjustments in preparation for a live satellite uplink. Bright floodlights had been set in place, powered by the onboard generator, and a camera operator had locked the outside broadcast camera onto the heavy metal tripod. A technician was making final checks to the cables and lighting, and the reporter, Joy Summers, was trying to get a handle on the story.

'Sorry, Officer, as I understand it you've been involved with this incident since it first broke?' Joe Barnes tried to be helpful.

'Yes, we've been working on it since early yesterday evening.' Joy Summers was scribbling notes on her clipboard.

'I see, and who exactly first raised the alarm?' Joe Barnes ran through the story to date, from when Steve Harper tried to find his daughter, Becky, at the holiday club to the latest discovery of the tent on the glacier and the note found at the refuge. The reporter jotted down the key points. In her head, she was already beginning to shape the story for the viewers. Joe Barnes just wanted to get the interview over with so that he could catch up on the latest progress from the search team.

At the rescue control centre, Rick Edwards, the team leader, had called a meeting to officially update everyone and plan the next stage of the search. Kate Jensen and the search team had returned from the glacier with the remains of the orange tent and the note found at the refuge. Ben and Becky's parents, Zoe's mum and Sam's dad had been there all day. Marcus' parents and Carla's mum had joined them when they heard the latest news about Marcus and Carla. The strain was beginning to show on their faces. Rick Edwards chose his words carefully.

'Right, we know the children have taken shelter on the glacier and it looks like they spent last night at the refuge. That's got to be good news.'

'So why have they not been found?' said Carla's mum. 'I just don't understand it.' Rick Edwards held up his hand and continued.

'Now, Kate Jensen and her team have checked out the direct route off the glacier down Shepherds' Gully and there's no sign of them.'

'Which means they must be still up there.' Marcus' dad found it hard to hide his frustration. 'Our children are still up there on the glacier and we're sitting down here unable to help them.' The team leader tried to sound positive.

'From what we know, your children have already done quite a lot to help themselves. That's a good sign. We have to remain hopeful.' Marcus' mum still needed answers.

'But where else on the glacier could they find shelter? Without shelter, they don't stand a chance.' Rick Edwards looked across at Sam's dad who was deep in thought.

'Well, Jack, what do you think? You've taken your son, Sam, walking on the glacier in the summer. Where do you think he would go?' Sam's dad looked up at the map on the wall.

'I think Sam would head for the nearest building he could find. If he has a compass and map with him, he'll find it.' Ben's dad seemed to agree.

'Yes, I reckon they've gone on from the refuge. I think they've tried to return across the glacier to Eagle Summit.'

'But Eagle Summit will be closed down,' said Zoe's mum. 'Even if they reached it, they wouldn't be able to get inside the building.'

'If they managed to reach it, I'd put my money on Sam being able to find a way in,' said Sam's dad.

'Okay,' said the team leader, 'for the time being we're going to assume they managed to reach Eagle Summit. It's dark now and visibility is poor. There's no more we can do tonight. I've checked the forecast and it looks as if the weather is set to improve slightly tomorrow. At first light we'll get a search team up to Eagle Summit.'

'Why can't they run the cable car tonight and see if they're there?' said Ben's mum. 'Surely, that would be easy enough?' Rick Edwards shook his head.

'If only we could. Unfortunately, there's a major fault on the lift system. The engineers are working on the problem but, for the time being, the only way up is on foot.'

'What about a helicopter?' said Ben's dad. 'Can't they fly over the glacier and Eagle Summit and take a look?' Rick Edwards nodded.

'That's an option, but only if the weather improves. The pilot will do his best to get airborne but he can't afford to take any risks. Now I suggest everyone tries to get some rest. We're going to need to save all our energies for tomorrow.' With that the meeting broke up. Things were serious but, at least, there was still hope.

Outside Forest Ridge Junior School, the crowd of onlookers had grown. Joy Summers, news reporter for the Skyline Television channel, was waiting patiently in the glare of the floodlights. Large flakes of snow drifted down around her.

'Stand by, everyone,' called the director in her earpiece, 'we're going live in ten, nine, eight, seven, six, five, four, three, two, one, and cue Joy …' Joy Summers looked up from her clipboard and into the lens of the camera.

'Good evening from the ski resort of Forest Ridge where we're gathered outside the local junior school. Only a few days ago, the children here were looking forward to an unexpected holiday after a freak accident damaged their school building. Now, the people of Forest Ridge are waiting for news as an even more dramatic story unfolds. Six local children are missing, somewhere on the mountain above this quiet village and, so far, search teams have been unable to find them.' The news reporter took a few steps to her left as the camera operator panned round to follow her. 'I'm joined now by Police Officer Joe Barnes from the Forest Ridge Police Department, who will hopefully be able to give us the latest news.' Joe Barnes stepped into the glare of the floodlights. 'Tell me, Officer Barnes, what is the latest news?' Joe Barnes cleared his throat.

'Well, the search team has managed to identify all the missing children on CCTV footage in Forest Ridge and Silver Lake and they are now following up those leads.'

Joy Summers nodded her head as she listened before continuing.

'And where, exactly, does the search team think the children are now?' Joe Barnes shuffled his feet uncomfortably.

'To the best of our knowledge, we have reason to believe the missing children may have spent the night at a refuge on the glacier but we are unsure of their present situation.' The director was now giving the news reporter a signal to wind up her live report so she moved back to her position in front of the school building for her final piece to camera.

'So, that's the situation here in Forest Ridge. The rescue services are doing all they can but, right now, there are still six children missing somewhere on the frozen mountain behind us, and their parents, and friends, can only hope and wait for news. This is Joy Summers, in Forest Ridge, for Skyline News. Now back to the studio.' After a few seconds, the director broke the silence.

'Okay, everyone, well done. Let's get packed up.'

The floodlights were switched off and the satellite uplink was terminated. Equipment was dismantled, and stored, and the crowd of onlookers melted away. The news team had done their job, and television viewers had been provided with a two minute slot about a drama unfolding in a local ski resort. Police Officer Joe Barnes was glad it was all over. He had done what was required of him, but he wondered if any of those watching the news report appreciated the seriousness of the situation. Tomorrow would be another day. He just hoped it would bring good news.

CHAPTER 16

In her dream, Zoe was back on the glacier, at the bottom of the crevasse. No matter how hard she tried, she couldn't get a foothold on the icy walls. She was trapped where no-one would find her, but suddenly she could hear a sound, somewhere high above her. Someone was crying faintly. Someone was calling her name. Zoe awoke with a start. It was dark and only one candle still flickered in its holder.

'Zoe, it's sore. It's really sore.' It was Becky crying, sitting up on the padded bench seat where she'd gone to sleep. Zoe got up and went across to her.

'What's the matter, Becky?'

'It's my ankle, it hurts. It really hurts.' Zoe fetched the candle from the table and held it over Becky's foot. It was very swollen and it didn't look good. Zoe thought what she could do. All the others seemed to be fast asleep, curled up in different parts of the Eagle's Nest Café.

'Listen, Becky,' said Zoe, 'I'm going to see if I can find something to make your ankle more comfortable. Try to keep still.' Through in the kitchen area, Zoe found a fresh candle. She lit it and pressed it into the candle-holder. If Zoe's ankle was broken it would need a splint, but what was she going to use?

'Can I help?' Marcus was standing at the kitchen door.

'It's Becky. She's in a lot of pain. I think her ankle may be broken. I'm looking for something I can use to make a splint.' Marcus had an idea.

'There are some cardboard boxes in the storeroom. I'll see what I can find.' Marcus disappeared through to the back. In one corner of the storeroom was a cardboard box containing paper hand towels. He emptied them out and brought the box through to the kitchen.

'Here,' he said, 'we can use this. There's a large pair of scissors in that drawer over there.' Zoe found the scissors and passed them to Marcus. He started to cut out one side of the box.

'We can make a splint out of this,' he said. 'If we can stop her ankle moving about, it should help ease the pain. Sit down in that chair so that I can get a measurement.' Zoe sat down and Marcus moulded the cardboard around her ankle, creasing it along the corrugated lines until he had a snug fit. 'There that should do the trick,' he said.

'Where did you learn to do that?' said Zoe. Marcus shrugged.

'Oh, just a little trick I learned on a First Aid course. See if you can find some padding and something to tie it in place.' Zoe started to search through the cupboards. She found a towel and an old table cloth.

'This should do,' she said. She passed Marcus the towel and snipped the edge of the table cloth with the scissors. She'd seen her mum do that when she wanted to tear a piece of cloth. Before long she had enough strips of material to bind the splint.

Back in the café, Becky was still whimpering. Zoe gently lifted her foot and Marcus carefully positioned the cardboard splint and tie strips under her ankle and padded it with the towel.

'Now lower her foot down slowly,' he said. Becky winced slightly as Zoe and Marcus bound the splint as tightly as they could around her ankle without hurting her. When they had finished, Becky's ankle was held firm and still. It was the best they could do. Marcus fetched a cushion from one of the café chairs, and together they raised her foot and slipped the cushion underneath. Becky seemed to have dozed off again so they crept back into the kitchen, with the candle, so as not to disturb her.

'I spotted something in the store cupboard,' said Marcus, 'and I could do with a hot drink.' He disappeared through the back and, when he returned, he had some sachets of hot chocolate and a sealed tin of assorted biscuits. 'Look what I've found,' he said, holding up the tin and the instant chocolate. 'Let's boil up some water.'

Ten minutes later, Zoe and Marcus were sitting either side of a serving unit, supping two steaming mugs of hot chocolate and munching biscuits. It was strange, sitting there in silence, in the light of the candle. It was Zoe who spoke first.

'Marcus, can I ask you something?' Marcus looked up. He wondered what was coming.

'If you want to,' he said. Zoe paused before continuing.

'Did you plan all this?' Marcus looked uncomfortable.

'What do you mean?' Zoe unzipped the pocket of her ski jacket and pulled out a map. It was Marcus' map, the one he had used to plan their journey from Eagle Summit to Silver Lake. Zoe carefully unfolded it and laid it out in the light of the candle. She said nothing as she slowly traced the red pen line with her finger all the way across the base of the glacier from Eagle Summit and down Shepherds' Gully into Silver Lake. Marcus was watching intently but he said nothing. She then ran her finger along the line of the funicular railway up to Glacier Station and paused. Marcus looked at her and then back down at the map, as Zoe followed the red pen line from Glacier Station back across the glacier to Eagle Summit. Marcus took another drink of his hot chocolate before speaking.

'Are you going to tell them?' he said. 'Are you going to tell them I planned it?'

'But why, Marcus, why did you do it?'

'You weren't all meant to be involved. It was just going to be Carla and me trying it, and then the plan went wrong - the cable car breaking down, Becky following us, and then missing the bus. I just wanted to prove a point.'

'But why, what do you have to prove?' Marcus thought for a moment before answering.

'It's alright for you. You're not going to have to move away and leave all your friends behind. They don't care what I think. They don't care how I feel. They don't care about me.'

'That's not true,' said Zoe. 'Of course your mum and dad care about you.'

'Then, why are they splitting up? If they cared about me, they wouldn't be splitting up.' Zoe folded up the map and pushed it to one side.

'Perhaps they're splitting up because they do care about you, because it's best for everyone. Why do you think my mum moved to Forest Ridge? It wasn't an easy decision for her, starting out on her own.' Marcus took the map in his hands, gripping it tightly.

'I just want them to listen to me, to start treating me like a grown up.'

'And you thought that by risking a journey across the glacier, and back again, you could prove that you could stand on your own two feet?' Zoe waited. 'Is that it?' Marcus looked at her and, then, slowly nodded his head. Zoe got up from her seat.

'Are you going to tell?' said Marcus.

'Tell?' said Zoe. 'No, I'm not going to tell. The question is, are you going to tell? At the moment, we're in this together and what's important is that everyone gets home safely.' And that's how their night time chat ended. Zoe took the hot chocolate mugs and washed them at the sink and Marcus went back through to the café and put two more logs on the fire. Everyone was still fast asleep and Becky had drifted off, her ankle held firmly in the cardboard splint. Marcus curled up on a bench in the corner and Zoe made herself as comfortable as she could on the floor beside Becky. Suddenly, she felt very tired, physically and mentally exhausted by everything that had happened to her. In a few minutes she was asleep and, this time, she didn't dream. She fell into a deep sleep that she would need to recharge her batteries, which was just as well because she was going to need all her strength for the challenge that lay ahead.

Ben was the first one to wake. For a moment, he couldn't work out where he was and, then, it all came flooding back to him. The fire had gone out and there was a chill in the air. Rolling out of his makeshift bed, he made his way across the Eagle's Nest Café to the door that led to the downstairs toilets. In the basement, daylight was filtering through a frosted window, reflecting off the coloured tiles on the walls. Ben ran some cold water into a wash hand basin and splashed it over his face to wipe the sleep from his eyes. It was freezing cold. Fortunately, there were some paper towels in a dispenser to dry himself. By the time he got back upstairs, the others were beginning to stir.

'What time is it?' said Sam.

'Time to get up,' said Ben. 'We need to make some decisions.' It was then that Ben noticed Becky's ankle, strapped up in the cardboard splint. He'd obviously slept through whatever had happened with Becky. Through in the kitchen he spotted the sachets of hot chocolate and the tin of biscuits, so he put on a pot of water to boil.

Slowly, one by one, the others joined him in the kitchen, all that is except Becky who was, fortunately, still asleep.

'When do you think they'll find us?' said Carla. Sam had been outside, checking on the weather.

'The sky is beginning to clear,' he said. 'With any luck, they'll have search parties out looking for us from first light. They may even be able to get the rescue helicopter into the air.'

'Can't we do something to attract their attention?' said Carla.

'Like what?' said Marcus.

'I don't know,' said Carla, 'but there must be something we can do.' Sam had an idea.

'We could always send up smoke signals.' Ben didn't know if he was being serious.

'Smoke signals?'

'Yes,' said Sam, 'we could have a look down in the basement switch room and see if we can find something to burn.' Before anyone could follow up Sam's suggestion, a loud squeal came from the café. They all rushed through to find Becky trying to sit up. She'd moved her foot and now her ankle was beginning to throb with pain.

'Marcus and I put the splint on last night,' explained Zoe. 'It was badly swollen. We think it may be broken.' Ben was clearly upset. Seeing his little sister in such pain made him anxious to do something.

'We're going to have to get help,' said Ben. 'We can't just leave her like this.'

'What about Sam's idea?' said Carla. 'Why don't we build up the fire and try to send up some smoke. Someone may spot it from down below.'

Urged on by Becky's crying, they all got to work. Sam and Ben made their way down to the basement to search for anything they could find that might burn and give off smoke. Marcus and Zoe got the fire going again whilst Carla brought Becky a hot drink and some biscuits to take her mind off her swollen ankle. When Sam and Ben returned, they had a bundle of oily rags and an old floor mat that might just do the trick. For the next hour, they fed the fire strips of rags and pieces of matting and Sam went outside to check how much smoke they were creating. It looked pretty black but there was no way he could tell if it would be seen from down below.

What was also worrying was that Becky had developed a dry cough as a result of being at high altitude. Ben knew he couldn't just wait any longer. For all they knew, it could be hours or even days before they were rescued.

'I'm going to have to go for help,' said Ben. 'I'm going to have to ski down to Crystal Rock and raise the alarm.'

'What are you talking about?' said Zoe. 'You can't ski down from here. You know the run's closed. It's too dangerous.' Ben had a look of determination on his face.

'I'll just have to give it a try,' he said. 'If there's only one way down, then that's what I have to do. I'll have to ski the Precipice run.'

CHAPTER 17

Outside the lift station at Crystal Rock, Kate Jensen and the search team were making final preparations. Each team member was wearing a transceiver to help with search and rescue. With her own device set to search, she checked that each piece of equipment was transmitting correctly and then she set her own transceiver to transmit. They were going into an area where the avalanche risk was high so there was no room for error.

'Okay, everyone,' said Kate Jensen, 'let's do one final equipment check.' Each team member carried an ice axe and folded steel probe. Once they had started up the side of the Precipice run, they would have to rely on the spiked crampons attached to their boots for grip. If the worst happened, and they lost their footing, only their ice axe could brake their fall and stop a treacherous slide down the steep face of the mountain. 'Right,' she said, 'let's get going.'

In silence, Kate Jensen led the search team away from Crystal Rock towards the foot of the Precipice run. From below, she could see that there had been another heavy build up of snow on the frozen layer beneath. The bond between the two layers would be weak and it wouldn't take much for the top layer to slide off. In any other situation this area would have been strictly off limits but, in the circumstances, they had little choice. Six children were missing and no-one knew what state they were in. They had to find them as soon as possible.

Progress was slow. As the gradient became steeper and steeper, the team had to pace themselves, sucking in all the thin air that was available at altitude. In places, the wind had scoured away the top layer of snow leaving only sheet ice. Those up front had to kick steps into the glassy slope for those following behind. It was a gruelling climb. Suddenly, Kate Jensen's radio crackled into life.

'Base to Rescue One, do you read me?' It was the voice of Rick Edwards, the search team leader. Kate

Jensen pressed the transmit button on the radio strapped to her shoulder.

'Go ahead, Rick,' she said, before releasing the transmit button. The rest of the team took a welcome rest.

'Heli-Med Air Support has confirmed that they hope to be airborne in the next thirty minutes so you should have air assistance if needed - over.'

'Understood, Rick. If the visibility is good enough, they could try flying over the glacier to see if they can spot anything - over.'

'Message understood, Kate. I'll pass it on. Oh, and just to let you know, someone has reported spotting some dark smoke over the summit. It's probably nothing but we'll check it out - over.' Kate Jensen looked up towards the summit but there was too much cloud to make anything out.

'Okay, thanks Rick - over and out.' Falling back into line the search team continued their ascent towards Eagle Summit. Little did they know that inside the Eagle's Nest Café, another drama was developing.

'But you can't, Ben,' said Zoe. 'I've told you it's too dangerous.' Ben Harper was adjusting the rear binding on his ski, the one he had lent to Marcus. He slid it forward and clamped down the heel of his boot. When he was satisfied with the fit, he snapped the toe binding free.

'I've got to, Zoe,' said Ben. 'I can't just leave Becky the way she is. I've got to try to get help.'

'Then, I'll have to come with you,' said Zoe. 'You can't go on your own.'

'Don't be stupid,' said Ben. 'There's no point in two of us taking a risk.' Ben sat down on one of the café chairs to put his boots on. Zoe sat down beside him.

'That's just the point. If you're on your own, you will be at risk. If something happens to you, no-one will know. At least if there are two of us, someone may be able to go for help.' Ben could see that Zoe was not going to give up.

'Alright,' he said, 'but don't blame me if we both get into trouble. It's your decision.' Ben and Zoe got their equipment together. Sam had to help Zoe to close her ski boots; the plastic shell of the boots had stiffened up

180

overnight, and he had to apply pressure to snap the buckles into place. They pulled on their safety helmets and gloved up, before carrying their skis and poles down to the basement switch room. All the others, except Becky, followed to see them off.

Outside in the morning air, it felt like minus ten but at least it had stopped snowing. A tiny glimmer of sunlight over to the east was beginning to burn off the low cloud. Carefully, they both cleaned the snow from the soles of their boots to ensure a secure fit and snapped on their skis. This was no time for a ski binding to accidentally release. Zoe pulled her ski goggles down from the front of her helmet and carefully adjusted them. Ben followed suit. He had carefully cleaned and dried the lenses to give himself the best possible view. They would both need it.

'Okay, are you ready?' said Ben. Zoe nodded.

'Ready, when you are,' she said. With a prod on their poles they slid forward, watched by the others as they glided around and under the lift cable before disappearing from view. The rest of the group retreated back indoors. All they could do now was wait.

When Ben and Zoe reached the top of the drop off point on the Precipice run they stopped. It was narrow, it was steep and it was a long way down.

'Well, there's no point in hanging around,' said Zoe. 'We may as well go for it.'

'Okay,' said Ben, 'let's take it nice and slowly.' Ben slid over the edge, keeping as much weight as possible over his downhill ski and Zoe followed in his tracks. The snow was deep as they ploughed a furrow through the dry powder. Ben went into a narrow snowplough, transferring his weight to the uphill ski to start the turn. As the tips of his skis pointed downhill, he gently transferred the pressure to turn across the slope and start a traverse in the opposite direction. Zoe followed his line and tucked in behind him. So far, it was going well and, every few turns, they paused to take a breather. Zoe led off on the next section. The slope was becoming wider and, with most of her weight over her downhill ski, she was able to hold her line on a long shallow traverse. Their descent of the Precipice run was slow, but at least it was controlled.

After about fifteen minutes, they stopped beside some rocks to take stock of their progress. There was still a long way to go and the next section looked even steeper.

'What do you think?' said Zoe. 'Do you think it's safe?' Ben wasn't sure.

'I think we should do this one at a time,' said Ben. 'I'll go first. You wait here until I'm across and then follow on.' Ben eased himself forward and Zoe waited by the rocks. When Ben was safely across, she started to traverse the slope, following in Ben's tracks. As her speed increased, she tried to edge her downhill ski in an attempt to slow herself. Suddenly, she caught an inside edge, splitting her skis and throwing her off balance. There was nothing she could do to stop it. In a second, she was spun around and one of her bindings broke free. Zoe tumbled forward and hit the slope, sliding down the steep face, before coming to a stop well below Ben.

'My ski,' she shouted. 'I've lost it.' Losing a ski on a normal run was a minor inconvenience. Losing it in deep snow, without a leash attached, was another matter. Ben climbed back up to the point where Zoe had fallen and poked around with his pole to see if he could find her ski.

There was no telling how far it could have travelled underneath the surface of the snow. Zoe also stepped back up the steep slope, searching in vain for the missing ski. It was hopeless. At last, exhausted, they sat down at the edge of the run.

'What do we do now?' said Zoe. 'I can't get down on only one ski. It's just too steep.' For a moment, Ben thought about giving Zoe one of his skis but even he knew that would be a challenge too far.

'You'll have to wait here, Zoe, until I get help. Will you be alright on your own?'

'I don't have a lot of choice,' said Zoe. 'You'll have to go for it. I'll be okay.' There was no point in wasting time. Ben headed back across the slope, descending as steeply as he dared. He had to keep going now if all their efforts were not to be wasted. He managed to make one more turn, and then it happened. A large crack suddenly opened up across the slope. One minute Ben was there slowly traversing the mountain and the next he was caught up in the rush of white powder. In front of her eyes, Zoe saw a great slab of snow break away and slide down the mountain with a roar, taking Ben with it. One minute he was there and, the next, he was gone. She didn't even have time to scream. She just sat there in the snow, watching the avalanche unfold, unable to take in what had just happened.

Suddenly, a roar filled her head, a great whirring sound that made the ground shake all around her. For a moment, she thought another avalanche would sweep her away as well but this sound was different. From overhead, there appeared a helicopter, swooping low in a wide arc. When it returned, she could see the faces of the pilot and the navigator. They came in low, hovering above her. Through the window the navigator held up his hand in a gesture that could only mean one thing - stay put. But Zoe had other things on her mind. Jumping to her feet, she pointed frantically in the direction where she had seen Ben disappear. The helicopter crew seemed, instinctively, to understand. The navigator gave her the okay sign by making a circle with his forefinger and thumb and the helicopter banked sharply away over the avalanche zone. Using their onboard detection radar, they flew systematically over debris field, searching for any response from beneath the snow. If the casualty had detection reflectors built into their clothing, or equipment, they might be able to pick up a signal. What Zoe didn't know was that the pilot had already sent out a distress call with the exact coordinates of the avalanche. Kate Jensen, and the search team, picked up the transmission and she quickly responded to the call.

'Heli-Med Air Support, this is Rescue One. We are in sight of the avalanche area now. Have you detected any reflector signals within the debris zone - over?' The radio crackled into life.

'Rescue One, this is Heli-Med Air Support - negative - we can detect no signals. We will try to land and provide search backup - over and out.' It was now a race against time.

As one, the search team switched their transceivers to search. If they were going to locate the casualty, they didn't want any stray transmissions. As they reached the bottom of the avalanche zone, they fanned out and started searching for any signal from beneath the snowpack. It was a long shot but any way to narrow the search would save valuable time. It soon became clear, however, that

186

whoever had triggered the avalanche hadn't been wearing a transceiver. They would have to search by hand.

Each team member unfolded the steel probe they carried and snapped the sections into place. Stretched out in a line they started to cross the debris field, pushing the search probes down into the snow. It was slow work but they had no choice. Each time they retracted the steel rods, they stepped forward and thrust them down again as far as they would reach, feeling for that telling resistance. As they worked, each team member knew that survival time was limited but they had to work systematically if they were to find the casualty. If only they had extra help.

Suddenly, they heard a loud bark. The helicopter team had found a landing spot and with them was a rescue dog, trained to sniff out any buried casualty in the fastest possible time. Kate Jensen knew the dog well. It was one of their best dogs.

'Here, boy, here, Max. Go search, go search.' Max bounded across the snow, his nose to the ground, hardly pausing as he zig-zagged back and forward across the slope, climbing higher each time. Suddenly, above them on the run, the large dog stopped, frozen to the spot, barking furiously and clawing at the snow. Kate Jensen held up her hand.

'Hold it, everyone. He's found something. Good boy, Max, good boy!'

CHAPTER 18

Beneath the snow, Ben Harper coughed to clear his airway. It was pitch-black and a very heavy weight was pressing down on him but, at least, in front of his face, there was a small air pocket. He tried to move but it was impossible. Where was he? What had happened? He felt drowsy and kept slipping in and out of consciousness. Was it a dream? Then, all of a sudden, he could hear something, a sound that was familiar. It was barking, a dog barking, his dog barking. It was Max!

Above him light appeared, at first only a glimmer, but it gave him hope and he was able to gulp in fresh air. He could also hear voices, excited voices. He could feel people digging around him, clawing at the snow with their hands. Then, at last, he could feel something touch his cheek, something licking furiously against his face to warm his chilled skin.

'Max,' said Ben, 'it's you, Max.'

From that point on, Ben Harper could only remember flashes of scenes, like an edited movie. The search team worked around him to protect his airway and check for injuries. The next thing he knew he was being lifted and something hurt. Wrapped in an insulation bag, he was lowered onto a field stretcher, his neck and head held firmly in a brace. Where were they taking him, he thought? Why couldn't he stand up? He drifted off again as the team carried him over difficult ground to the waiting helicopter. His arm was really hurting now. Around him he could hear a loud whirring noise that grew louder and louder. He opened his eyes to see what was happening. He was attached to something, tightly strapped in, unable to move and, then, they were off.

The helicopter lifted slowly into the air, climbing away from the mountain at increasing speed, with the stretcher held firmly in a cradle on the side of the aircraft. The voice of the pilot was already radioing ahead.

'Base, this is Heli-Med Air Support. We have the casualty safely on board and are heading for Bridgeton Accident Unit. Please advise that our expected time of

190

arrival is fifteen minutes.' Ben looked up one last time. A face was looking down at him, monitoring his condition. He tried to recognise who it was but they were wearing a helmet, microphone and visor. Slowly, he closed his eyes and drifted off into a deep sleep. It had been a busy day and now it was time to rest.

Back on the mountain, the drama was not yet over. There were still five more children to be rescued. Stowing their equipment, the search team continued their climb up the side of the Precipice run. They kept silent and tried to cause as little disturbance as possible. The slope had already avalanched once. They didn't want to set off another one. By the time they reached Zoe, she was numb with the cold and also with the shock of seeing Ben disappear.

'Is he alright?' she said. 'Is Ben alright?' Kate Jensen tried to reassure her.

'He should be fine,' she said. 'Now let's see about getting you down safely.' There was no way Zoe would have the strength to climb back up to Eagle Summit and the helicopter was down in Bridgeton. They had to get her off the mountain as soon as possible before hypothermia set in.

One of the team undid a set of skis lashed to each side of his backpack. He was the team member experienced in extreme skiing and he carried a spare pair of ski boots for just such an emergency. He had skied some of the most dangerous slopes on the mountain, carving turns down rocky gullies and over steep cliffs. For him, the Precipice run was just a minor challenge. Hoisting Zoe up onto his back, he got her to hold tightly around his neck.

'Here we go,' he said. 'Cling on.' Heading off down the slope, he bounced through the deep powder snow with seemingly effortless ease, swinging from edge to edge in a steady, flowing rhythm. Behind them, they left a long, snaking furrow in the unbroken snow as they progressed steadily towards the bottom of the run. Zoe clung on tightly, at times almost too scared to keep her eyes open, but, at last, the slope began to level out. They were down safely. To Zoe's surprise, there was an unexpected welcoming party. She was quickly transferred to the warm cabin of a Snowcat machine for the next part of the journey across to the Crystal Rock lift station. From there they would take her for a medical checkup and a reunion with her mum, but Zoe couldn't help but think about the others still trapped up at Eagle Summit. If the cable car was broken, how would they all get down?

Once they had repacked their equipment, the search team headed on up the mountain towards Eagle Summit. They kept to the side of the Precipice run for fear of triggering another avalanche. The higher they climbed, the steeper it got and it wouldn't take much disturbance for another slab of ice and snow to break away. It was almost noon by the time they reached the top lift station. Kate Jensen had a set of keys for the Eagle Summit structure so she was able to open the main entrance door and gain access. The team fanned out to search the building for any sign of the other children. At first the place seemed empty but, then, they came upon a pair of skis and a set of wet footprints leading to the connecting door to the Eagle's Nest Café. Kate Jensen opened it slowly and stepped inside.

'Any chance of a coffee?' she said. The faces of four children stared back at her, at first unable to speak.

'We've been found,' whispered Carla. 'We've been found.' Then, all at once, the children regained their voices and they all wanted to speak at the same time.

'What about Ben and Zoe?' said Marcus. 'Did they make it?'

'Are they alright?' said Sam. 'We waited and waited and we thought no-one was coming.' Kate Jensen held up her hand to calm them all down.

'Yes, they'll be fine,' she said, 'once they've had a chance to recover. Now what about the rest of you? Is everyone okay?' Carla stepped forward.

'It's Becky,' she said. 'She's hurt her ankle. We think it may be broken.' Kate Jensen had spotted Becky lying on a bench seat in the corner.

'Well, let's have a look,' she said. 'I see someone has been looking after her.'

'Marcus and Zoe did it,' said Carla. 'They made her a splint. They didn't know what else to do.' Kate Jensen was gently checking Becky's ankle. Becky called out in pain.

'You've done a good job. Well done,' she said, 'but I think we need to get her to hospital as soon as possible. Her foot is badly swollen.'

'But how are we going to get back down?' said Sam. 'Will they send a helicopter for us?' Kate Jensen knew that might not be so easy.

'We'll come up with something,' she said. 'Now whilst I'm on the radio, why don't you children see if you can make some hot drinks for my team.' As they all disappeared into the kitchen for mugs of hot chocolate, Kate Jensen made her way outside to get a better radio signal.

'Rescue One to Base, do you read me - over?' She didn't have long to wait.

'Go ahead, Kate, any news?'

'Yes,' she said, 'most of the children seem fine but the youngest one needs to get her ankle set as soon as possible. What's the position with Heli-Med Air Support? Can they get back up here to evacuate the casualty?'

'The helicopter is still down in Bridgeton. They'll need to refuel so it could take some time.' Kate Jensen was keen to get all the children off the mountain as soon as possible. It would take quite a few air lifts to get them all back down to Forest Ridge.

'What about the cable car? Is there any news on that?' she asked.

'Yes, they think they may have solved the problem but the engineers would still need to give it a test run. I'll check with them and get back to you.'

'If you could,' she said. 'The sooner we get the children and the search team back down to safety the better. We don't want to be stuck up here all night.' Kate Jensen went back inside to join the others. Carla handed her a mug of hot chocolate.

'Thank you,' she said, 'I could do with that.'

'Will they be able to get us down the mountain?' said Carla. Before Kate Jensen could answer, her radio crackled into life again.

'Base to Rescue One, do you read me?' Kate Jensen pressed the transmit button.

'Go ahead, Base.'

'It's good news. The engineers are ready to test the cable car. They'll restore power to the drive mechanism and send an operator up to you in the next few minutes. If there are no problems, we should have you all down in no time. Good luck.'

Everyone made their way through to the lift station and up the stairs to the control room. Kate Jensen used the keys to get inside. Outside the plate glass window they could see the top cable car hanging in the loading bay. Above the cabin the great steel hanger frame rested on two thick cable support wires. These took the weight of the cable car as it rode up and down the mountain. In between was the steel haul rope that would drag the cable car when it was ascending, or descending, between Crystal Rock and Eagle Summit.

Suddenly, the power in the control room came on and the control panels and screens lit up. A warning bell sounded and the huge pulley wheel began to turn. The top cable car gave a shudder and, very slowly at first, it started to pull away from the top station. As it descended, its weight would help to counter-balance the bottom cable car that was now being dragged up the mountain to join them. The children watched as it dropped away, the rotating carriage wheels riding over the top of the two support cables. Half way down, the two cable cars passed, the top one empty, the bottom one carrying the operator. So far, the test was going well and the engineers down below were satisfied with their repair work. The speed control system was functioning normally, the panel lights were as expected, and they were confident that they had resolved the fault.

Up top, the children watched as the lower cable car approached. As it neared the lift station, the speed of the motor was reduced and the steel drag rope began to slow. To avoid any damage to the cable car, or the loading bay, its speed reduced to a crawl as it pulled into Eagle Summit.

'Right,' said Kate Jensen, 'I'd like everyone to collect their gear and get ready for the journey down.' They all disappeared to collect their equipment. Four members of the search team lifted Becky carefully onto a stretcher that they'd located in the lift station. They carried her out to the loading bay where they were greeted by the cable car operator and placed her on the floor of the cabin. The rest of the children, and the search team, then joined them on board. Kate Jensen had made a final check of the building and secured the doors.

The cable car operator was in touch with the bottom lift station, at Crystal Rock, using a telephone handset on the cabin control panel. When everyone was safely aboard, he closed the sliding doors and notified the engineers down below to release the safety brake and power up the haul cable. A buzzer sounded and they started to move. They were on their way. Marcus, Carla and Sam moved up to the front to watch their descent through the front window. It was scratched and scraped from the many pairs of skis that had rested against it. It was hard to believe their ordeal was nearly over.

Halfway down, they passed the empty cable car climbing back up to Eagle Summit. They were travelling at speed now, racing down towards Crystal Rock. Suddenly, a warning alarm sounded. All the children look around to see what was happening. The cable car operator was talking hurriedly into the onboard telephone handset. He looked worried.

'What's happening?' said Sam. 'Why are we speeding up?' Sam knew this shouldn't be happening. The cable car had an automatic braking system if anything should go wrong but, as they approached the bottom lift station, they weren't slowing; they were speeding up. The operator hung up his handset, the panic-stricken voices of the engineers down below still ringing in his ears. Reaching up he grabbed a small handle above his head and shouted out his instructions.

'Everyone, get down on the floor! Get down on the floor and brace yourselves!'

CHAPTER 19

Inside the lift station at Crystal Rock, the test engineers had to act quickly. There had been a serious malfunction. The speed regulation device had failed and the cable car was hurtling towards them, out of control. The chief engineer thought fast.

'I'm cutting the power to the main drive shaft,' he shouted. 'Everyone stand clear.' He then grabbed the communication phone and gave his instructions to the operator inside the cable car.

'Emergency brake, emergency brake, apply the emergency brake!'

Inside the cabin, the operator pulled down sharply on the metal handle above his head. Up above the cable car, the brake assembly clamped down on the two cable support wires with a screech of metal on metal. From below the chief engineer could see sparks flying from the top of the cable car hanger frame.

'Come on,' he said to himself, 'do your job, slow down, brake.' Nothing seemed to be happening. The brakes were biting but the cable car was still travelling too fast.

Inside the cable car, all the children just covered their heads in fear. The whole cabin was shaking as the emergency brake pads gripped the support cables. The operator stood at his post, his hand firmly on the brake handle watching the fast approaching lift station. The cable car shuddered and swayed and, then, with a deafening squeal, it decelerated rapidly and came to a sudden halt. Everyone just lay there on floor, hardly daring to look. The cable car swung gently, suspended in the wind. One by one, they all got to their feet and looked downhill. They had stopped just a short distance from the bottom station loading bay. A voice sounded on the cable car speaker system. It was the chief engineer.

'Okay, everyone,' he said, 'the excitement's over. We have everything under control. Welcome back to Crystal Rock. I'm sorry if your journey back down was a little rough.' Inside the control room, the engineers switched to the backup drive system, the emergency brake was released and the cable car was able to crawl slowly into the loading bay under auxiliary power. The doors slid open and everyone filed out onto the metal grid decking that led into the bottom lift station. Becky was carried quickly to a waiting helicopter and flown directly to the main accident unit at Bridgeton. Carla wanted to go with her but there wasn't enough room. Instead, Marcus, Carla and Sam were all ushered away to a waiting Snowcat machine to take them down to Sugar Bowl where they transferred to the gondola lift for the final stage down to Forest Ridge. A small crowd had gathered and there seemed to be cameras and reporters everywhere. It was all overwhelming. Fortunately, the local police got them into a waiting minibus and drove them down to the Forest Ridge Medical Centre for a checkup. No-one spoke. So much had happened to them in just two days, it was difficult to know what to say or where to begin. At least, no-one bothered them with too many questions about their adventure. The doctors seemed quite surprised that, apart from a few bumps and bruises, they all seemed to be fit and well. It was Sam who wanted some answers.

'What about Ben, and Zoe and Becky?' he asked. 'Are they alright?' One of the doctors tried to reassure them.

'I'm sure they'll be alright. We'll see about that tomorrow. In the meantime, you've all had a very lucky escape. Now I think you should all go home as soon as possible.'

Sam's dad, Carla's mum and Marcus' parents were already waiting in the Medical Centre reception area. The strain of the last two days, and lack of sleep, still showed on their faces but their broad smiles said more than anything. It was Marcus' dad who spoke for them all.

'I'm sure you've all got plenty to tell us but, perhaps, we should leave that for another time, when we've all recovered.' With that, and a shake of hands, they went their separate ways. There would be so much to tell but, for now, all they wanted was a hot meal, a warm bath and a soft bed. Tomorrow would be soon enough.

Steve and Sue Harper stayed late into the evening at the Bridgeton Accident Unit. Their son Ben had suffered a fractured arm but, more importantly, he had survived an avalanche and not many people do that. He had been placed in a side room for observation but, as far as they could tell, he hadn't suffered any other damage. Their daughter, Becky, had been taken to a children's ward. Her ankle was broken and was now in a plaster cast but, in time, it would mend. Steve and Sue Harper took turns by their bedsides until midnight, by which time Ben and Becky were both sound asleep. One of the shift doctors met them both at a coffee machine in the reception area.

'Look, why don't you two go home and get some sleep. You could do with it. They're going to take some looking after over the next few days so you're going to need all your strength.' Sue Harper was uncertain what to do.

'I'm not sure I want to leave them,' she said. 'What if they wake up and we're not here?' The doctor tried to reassure her.

'Trust me,' he said, 'they'll be fine. You'll be of much more use to them after a good night's sleep. We'll phone you if there's any change.' So that's what they decided to do. Steve and Sue Harper drove back up the mountain to Forest Ridge, hopeful that everything was going to be alright. They needn't have worried.

The following morning, Ben and Becky's parents returned to Bridgeton. It was a bright, sunny day and there was hardly a cloud in the sky. Inside the Accident Unit, they reported to reception and were allowed to go straight through to the side room where they had left Ben. He was already sitting up in bed, proudly displaying the plaster cast on his arm like a battle trophy and there, on the end of the bed, was Becky.

'Look,' she said, 'they gave me crutches to get around.' At this, Becky hoisted herself up and started to hop around the room, much to the amusement of Ben who thought she looked like a pirate. His dad was clearly relieved.

'Well, you two seem to have recovered. You'll both be skiing again in no time.' Sue Harper wasn't so sure.

'We'll have to talk about that,' she said. 'I'm not letting either of you out of my sight until you've both fully recovered and I know exactly where you are.'

Outside the room there was a knock on the door. It was Zoe and her mum. They hadn't come empty handed. Zoe had a big box of chocolates and her mum had a basket of fruit. Ben could get used to being in hospital.

'Just what I need,' he said. 'I only had toast for breakfast.'

'I didn't,' said Becky. 'I had a boiled egg.' They all laughed.

For the next thirty minutes, they all chatted and joked about the hospital and school and the holidays. Strangely, no-one mentioned their narrow escape. It was almost as if they were not ready to talk about what had happened and why. When the doctor came by to check on how they were, he could see that they had recovered from their ordeal. It was Becky who asked the question.

'When can we go home?' she said. The doctor glanced at the chart on the end of Ben's bed.

'Well,' he said, 'I can't see any reason why you can't both go home today. That's if your parents will have you.' Becky gave a whoop of delight.

'That's what I hoped you'd say.'

By lunchtime, they were all ready to leave the Accident Unit and head back up the mountain to Forest Ridge. It was strange driving up the twisting road, amongst all the other cars, heading for the slopes to take advantage of the fine weather. It all seemed so normal and it made Ben want to get his skis out and get back on the mountain. And then he remembered, he had a broken arm and his skis were buried in the snow somewhere up on the Precipice run. Maybe someone would find his skis, and Zoe's, when the snow thawed in the summer.

As they pulled into the village, his dad spoke.

'There's something I think we should do before going home,' he said. He stopped the car outside the Forest Ridge Community Centre and parked up.

'What are we going to do?' said Ben. 'Why have we come here?' His dad looked around from the front seat of the car.

'There are some people we have to thank, Ben. It's all arranged. Don't worry, I'll do the talking.'

Inside the Community Centre, it was strangely quiet. There didn't seem to be anyone about. They crossed the foyer, pulled open the doors to the main hall and stepped inside. Suddenly, a great cheer went up and everyone inside began to clap. Marcus, Carla and Sam were already inside and Zoe joined them. They seemed really glad to see him again, relieved that he only had a broken arm and nothing worse. Ben was confused. There were all sorts of people there from the village, some he hardly knew. His dad raised his arm to quieten the gathering. A hush fell on the hall and then he spoke.

'I would just like to thank all of you for supporting our families over the last few days. We couldn't have got through it all without you.' He paused for a moment, gathering his thoughts, choosing carefully what he wanted to say before continuing. 'I would especially like to thank the members of the search team for finding our children and bringing them safely down from the mountain. Thank you all.' Everyone applauded and the local mayor invited everyone to enjoy the celebration party. Ben could hardly believe it. What had he done to deserve it? What had any of them done to deserve a party?

For the next hour everyone circulated, talking excitedly and enjoying the celebration party. Marcus, Carla, Zoe and Sam all made sure they signed Ben and Becky's plaster casts with little pictures and messages. Everyone seemed to be having a great time but Ben wasn't. He felt strangely empty. His dad spotted him sitting on his own in the corner and went to join him.

'So, Ben, what's bothering you? Aren't you glad to be home?' Ben was unsure what to say.

'Yes,' he said, 'of course I am. It's just, I don't think I … we deserve it.'

'And why is that?' His dad wanted to get to the bottom of how he felt.

'Well, because we did wrong. We skied out of bounds and caused everyone a lot of worry and put other people at risk.' His dad thought for a minute.

'Did you mean to do it?' Ben thought about this.

'No, of course not. It just happened and one thing led to another.'

'Unfortunately, Ben, things don't always go as we plan them. Accidents happen even when we think it's safe, like the avalanche that damaged the school or the fault on the cable car. Even experts can get it wrong sometimes, you know.' This made Ben feel a bit better but there was still something that was worrying him.

'Will we lose our lift passes? Will they confiscate our season ticket?' His dad didn't answer immediately. He was thinking what to say.

'Well, of course, they have to have rules, don't they? They can't have people skiing out of bounds, without an experienced guide. That's important for everyone's safety.' Ben could only nod. They had broken the rules even if it wasn't really their fault. His dad continued. 'Then again, it's only when things go wrong that we learn from our mistakes, like the tree going through your classroom roof. They'll make pretty sure they upgrade the avalanche barriers so there's no chance of that happening again.'

'So what can we do to make sure it doesn't happen again?' said Ben. 'What can we do to make things safer for other skiers?' His dad thought for a moment.

'I think you, and Becky, and all the others can make skiing safer. There aren't many children who have survived what you have and come through it. You've all got a story to tell and it may just be worth allowing you, and the others, to hang on to your lift passes.' Ben was, suddenly, cheered up.

'Do you mean that? Do you think we will still be able to ski?'

'Oh, I think so,' said his dad, 'provided you keep your side of the bargain.'

CHAPTER 20

Three weeks after the huge fir tree fell through the roof of Ben's classroom, Forest Ridge Junior School reopened. To mark the occasion, all the children gathered in the main hall for a whole school assembly. Ben had to keep his plaster cast on for another couple of weeks but his mum said that was no reason to miss school. He could still write with his good arm. Everyone in the class wanted to know about their adventure.

'Zoe, how did you find your way across the glacier?'

'What was it like to be buried by an avalanche, Ben?'

'Sam, is it true the cable car almost crashed?' They were glad when the school Principal came into the hall and asked everyone to quieten down. After welcoming the children back for the new term, he announced that they had some special visitors to introduce.

'I would like you all to give a warm welcome to representatives of the Forest Ridge Search and Rescue Unit.' Everyone clapped as in walked Rick Edwards and Kate Jensen from the search team and - Ben could hardly believe it - his dad, Steve Harper, from the Ski Patrol. When the clapping had died down, the Principal continued. 'Now, as you may know, some children from our school recently had a bit of an adventure on the mountain and had a very lucky escape.' Everyone went very quiet. One or two children started to turn around to look towards the back of the hall. Ben, Zoe and Sam began to feel nervous because they didn't know what was coming. 'You may remember, before the holidays, we also had a lucky escape. Can anyone remember what happened?' The Principal pointed to one of the little ones who was waving her hand in the air.

'A big tree fell through the roof.'

'That's right but, fortunately, no-one was hurt and it has now been fixed. We have a nice new roof. Sometimes accidents happen and we just have to repair the damage. During the holidays, four of our children got lost on the mountain. It wasn't really their fault but they

214

had to deal with their mistake. They had to stick together, help each other and find their way home.' Ben, Zoe and Sam could feel their faces beginning to go red. 'I would now like to ask Ben and Becky Harper, Zoe Roberts and Sam Fletcher to come out to the front.' Ben, Zoe and Sam got slowly to their feet and started to make their way, reluctantly, to the front of the hall. Becky was sitting on a chair at the side and, with the aid of her crutches, she hopped to the front to join them. They all wondered what was coming. The Principal concluded. 'Now, I would like to pass you over to Mr Rick Edwards who led the search for the children.' Rick Edwards stepped forward.

'Thank you. As you know boys and girls, the Ski Patrol is very keen to make sure everyone enjoys skiing and snowboarding on the mountain. That's what we're here for. We want you all to have a great time and we want you to enjoy it safely. Most of you will never have an accident, and you may never get into trouble on the mountain; but the best way to stay safe is to know about the dangers and what can go wrong. And who better to hear it from than some of your own friends here in Forest

Ridge Junior School who have experienced it at first hand.' Rick Edwards turned to Kate Jensen. 'Kate, would you like to explain?' Kate Jensen stepped forward to speak.

'We would like to appoint four of your school friends as junior, assistant members of the Forest Ridge Ski Patrol. Their job will be to make sure all the children in the school know how to stay safe on the mountain. Firstly, Zoe Roberts.' Zoe stepped forward and shook Kate Jensen's hand and Steve Harper handed her a certificate. 'Next, Ben Harper and Sam Fletcher.' Everyone clapped as Ben and Sam received their certificates. Kate Jensen paused for a moment. 'Have we forgotten anyone?' Everyone called out.

'Becky!' Kate Jensen pretended to have forgotten.

'Oh yes, of course, Becky Harper.' Becky hopped forward, beaming. She even started giggling when her dad handed her a certificate and gave her a kiss on the cheek. All the children laughed and the assembly finished with a round of applause. Zoe, Ben, Sam and Becky rejoined their classes and all the children filed out of the hall and back to their classrooms. Everyone in the top class was still keen to know about everything that had happened when they were lost on the mountain. Their teacher, Ms Curtis, tried to get them all to settle down. Eventually, calm was restored.

'I think,' she said, 'we should all give Zoe, Ben and Sam a chance to settle back into their school work without all these questions. However, I know you are all keen to hear about their adventure so I have a suggestion to make.' All the children were listening now. 'I think we should get Zoe, Ben and Sam to spend some time at home writing down what they remember most about their adventure. When they're ready and prepared, we will let them tell us all about it, in their own words. Is that agreed?' All the children agreed, even Ben and Zoe, although Sam wasn't too sure at first. In some ways, it was good to get back to school, to get back to normality. It's exciting to have an adventure so long as it's not too frightening and you stay in control.

After school Ben, Zoe and Sam made their way to the centre of the village to watch the skaters on the outdoor ice rink. They never did get a chance to try it out during the holidays, or the swimming pool. It's strange how things you plan don't always work out. As they passed Phil and Angela King's Sports Store, they stopped to look at the latest skis in the window. Ben and Zoe were reminded that their skis were buried under the snow somewhere up on the Precipice run. Sam still had his second hand pair which he didn't mind. His dad couldn't afford to waste money on expensive skis like the ones in the window. As they were standing looking at the window display, Marcus' dad came out.

'Ah,' he said, 'just the people I'm looking for. Do you mind coming inside for a moment?' They all went inside the ski store. It was quiet. Phil King wasn't sure where to begin. 'I'd just like to say sorry, and thank you, for all you did.' They weren't sure what to say. 'Marcus has told me what happened. He has told me how he planned to cross the glacier and return from Glacier Station. Without you three with him, there's no telling what would have happened.' Zoe spoke up.

'He was upset, Mr King. He wasn't thinking straight.' Marcus' dad bit his lip.

'Yes, I know that. I guess his mum and I were too busy with other things. Anyway, that's behind us now.

Sometimes we don't know what we have until we almost lose it but I suppose you're still too young to know that.'

'No,' said Zoe, 'I understand.' Marcus' dad suddenly remembered what he wanted to say.

'Your skis,' he said. 'I hear you've lost your skis.'

'Yes,' said Ben, 'but they may turn up when the snow melts.' Phil King interrupted.

'I'd like you all to accept a new pair of skis from me, as a thank you present. I have to make room for new stock so I want you to take your pick.' Marcus' dad led them through to the ski section of the store and they all followed in silence. When they saw the range of the latest carving skis, all in dazzling colours, their eyes widened.

'But I've still got my skis,' said Sam. Marcus' dad was insistent.

'Please, Sam, choose a new pair. It's my way of saying thank you. It's alright, I've cleared it with your parents.'

It didn't take Ben, Zoe and Sam long to choose. They had done enough wishful, window-shopping to know the ones they wanted. Phil King set their chosen skis aside.

'That's sorted then. I'll fit bindings to them over the next few days and you can bring in one of your ski boots so I can correctly adjust the settings.' When they had all thanked him, they left the ski store, hardly believing their good fortune. This was something they had to celebrate so they made their way up to the Edelweiss Restaurant. They each bought an ice-cream fruit sundae and sat down at their favourite table in the corner. Zoe's mum spotted them and came over.

'Well,' she said, 'what's all this in aid of?' Zoe was almost too excited to speak.

'Marcus' dad has given each of us a new pair of skis as a thank you present.' Her mum nodded.

'Yes, I know,' she said. 'I tried to tell him it wasn't necessary but he was very insistent. I think it's very generous of him. Have you seen this?' Zoe's mum had a copy of the local newspaper under her arm. She laid it down on the table in front of them. Ben opened it out and there on the front cover was a picture of Marcus and Carla getting into the police minibus on the day they were rescued. However, it wasn't the front page picture that grabbed their attention. It was the headline. Ben read it out.

'New Ski Run for Forest Ridge.' Zoe was keen to know more. She took the newspaper from Ben and read on.

'Plans are in place to create a new ski run to link the resorts of Forest Ridge and Silver Lake. It will start at Eagle Summit and head across the base of the glacier and down Shepherds' Gully to Silver Lake. The run is expected to be completed for the start of next season. The idea for the run was inspired by the misadventure of a group of school children who completed the route following a fault on the Eagle Summit cable car. A spokesperson for the Ski Patrol said they felt this was the best way to prevent any further mishaps and to provide a useful link between the two resorts. Plans for a safe return across the glacier from Glacier Station to Eagle Summit are still under consideration.' When Zoe had finished reading, her mum drew their attention to a related article in a box at the bottom of the page.

'You may also be interested in this,' she said. Sam read out the details.

'The Forest Ridge Gazette is holding a competition to choose a name for the new run. Entries, with your name and address and the reason for your choice, should be sent to the newspaper's central office.'

'There,' said Zoe's mum, 'I'm sure you three could come up with a good name for the new run. I'll leave you to think about it.' As they finished off their ice-cream fruit sundaes, they all racked their brains to think of a name but nothing seemed to be quite right. Then, all of a sudden, Ben had an idea.

'I know what we could call it. It's something no-one else will think of.'

'What?' said Zoe. Ben paused to add to the suspense. Sam was impatient.

'Quickly, Ben, tell us. What could we call the new run?' Ben smiled.

'We could call it Skigos Way.'

It had been a very eventful day but when Ben got home from school, there was another surprise waiting for him. Outside his house was a large, four wheel drive car with

Skyline Television News painted on the side. His mum was standing talking to news reporter, Joy Summers, and a camera assistant was filming the interview. When they spotted Ben, they broke off from filming. Joy Summers seemed delighted to see him.

'Ah, and this must be your son, Ben,' she said. 'We've been waiting for you.' Ben wasn't quite sure whether he wanted to stay or run away. Unfortunately, before he had time to decide, Joy Summers had placed him in front of the camera and stuck a microphone under his chin.

'Tell me,' she said, 'how does it feel to be one of the youngest people to have survived an avalanche?' Taken by surprise, Ben said the first thing that came into his head.

'I feel pretty lucky, I guess.' The news reporter then went on to ask him a number of other questions which Ben answered as best he could. He was glad when his dad arrived home with his pet dog, Max. This gave Joy Summers the opportunity for some shots of Ben and Max playing together. Max and Ben chased each other around the garden before they both went tumbling, and rolling, in the snow. The reporter was sure the viewers would love it. There were just a few more shots they needed to complete her news report.

Skyline Television News had decided to present Ben's pet dog, Max, with a special award, on behalf of their viewers. The camera assistant filmed the news reporter presenting Max with a framed certificate for saving Ben's life and then they got a big close up of Max giving Ben a friendly lick on the cheek. The crew had to try three or four times before they got just the shot they wanted. All that was left was for Joy Summers to do her final piece to camera.

'So, this is one tale that really did have a happy ending, all thanks to a very special rescue dog, with a very special nose and tail, all of his own - this is Joy Summers, in Forest Ridge, for Skyline News.'

The news report was complete. They had all the camera footage they needed so they loaded the equipment into their car and set off back down the mountain road to the television studios in Bridgeton. There the story was edited into a three minute slot to be broadcast, the same evening, on the Skyline Television News.

That night, Ben and Becky and their mum and dad all tuned in to watch the news report about Max's special award. Becky was thrilled, Sue and Steve Harper were very proud, Ben watched it from behind a cushion and Max slept through it all.

After supper, Ben went up to his bedroom. He had decided he wanted to make a start on his story of their adventure up on the glacier so that he could share it with all the children in his class. Max, his pet dog, lay on the rug next to him watching his every move.

'Tell me, Max, what do you think would be a good title for my adventure story?' Max looked up at him with wide eyes. Until Ben had a title, it was difficult to begin his story. He took a bite out of the biscuit that lay on the plate on his desk. Max watched the crumbs fall from the biscuit and gave a small whimper, whilst licking his lips.

'No, I'm sorry, Max, I can't give you any of this. You know it's not good for you.' Max got up and placed his head on Ben's lap, looking up at him with pleading eyes. Ben began to waver. This was the dog that had recently saved his life. He had a framed certificate, hanging on the bedroom wall, to prove it and Ben wasn't prepared to give him even a little piece of biscuit.

'Oh, alright then,' said Ben, 'just a little bit but don't tell anyone I gave it to you.' Ben got Max to beg and popped the last piece of biscuit into his mouth. 'Now,' he said, 'what shall I call my story?' Max looked straight at Ben, as if urging him to come up with a good title. Then, out of the blue, it came to him.

'I know,' said Ben. 'I know what I'll call my story. I'll call it … **Out of Bounds**.'